CELTIC MYTHOLOGY FOR KIDS

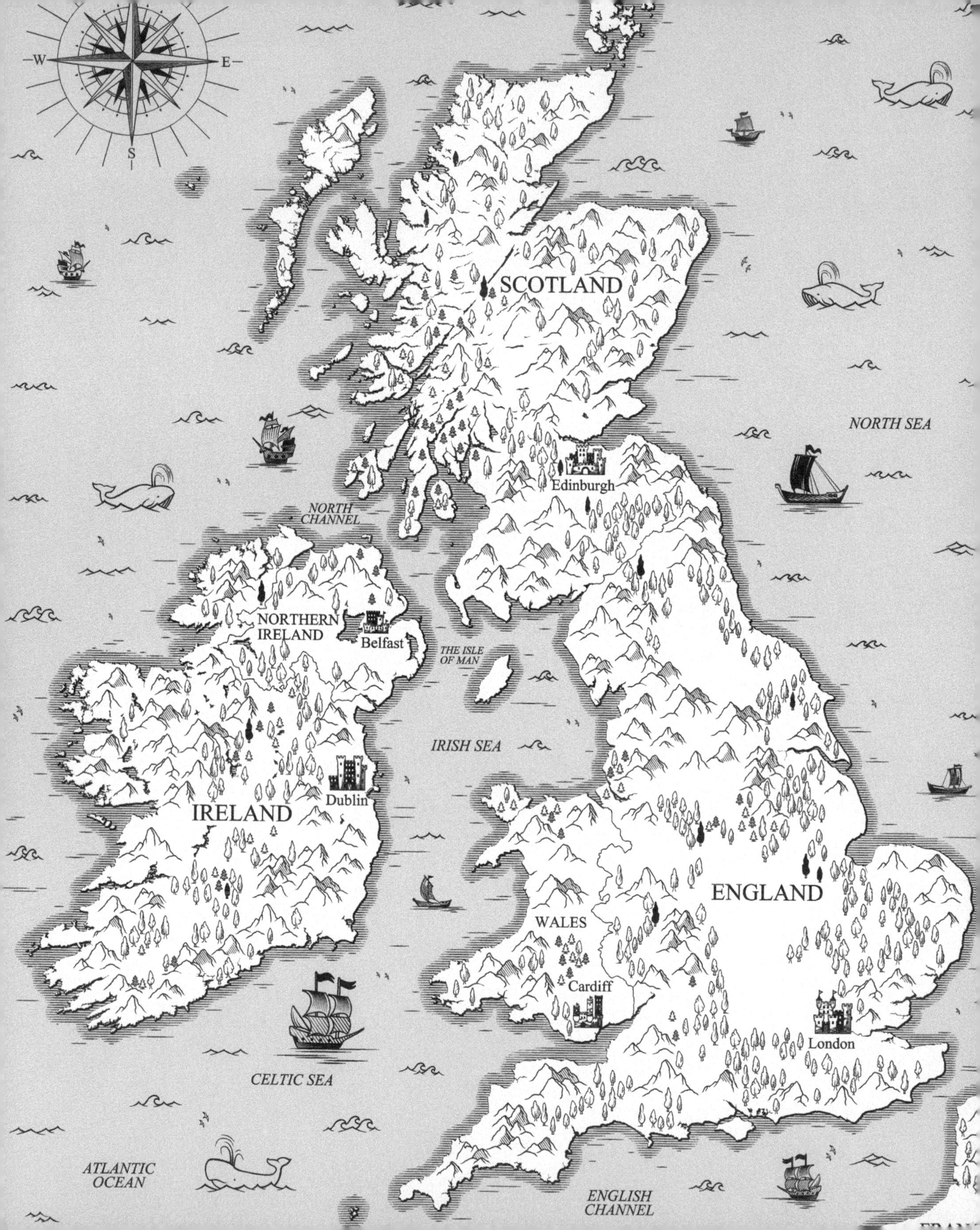
W
E
S
SCOTLAND
NORTH SEA
Edinburgh
NORTH CHANNEL
NORTHERN IRELAND
Belfast
THE ISLE OF MAN
IRISH SEA
Dublin
IRELAND
ENGLAND
WALES
Cardiff
London
CELTIC SEA
ATLANTIC OCEAN
ENGLISH CHANNEL

CELTIC MYTHOLOGY

FOR KIDS

TALES OF SELKIES, GIANTS, AND THE SEA

CHRISTOPHER S. PINARD

ILLUSTRATIONS BY JAVIER OLIVARES

ROCKRIDGE
PRESS

Interior and Cover Designer: John Clifford

Art Producer: Samantha Ulban

Editor: Jesse Aylen

Production Editor: Nora Milman

Illustrations by © 2020 Javier Olivares. All other images used under licence © Shutterstock.

ISBN: Print 978-1-64611-626-3 | eBook 978-1-64611-627-0

R0

For my mother,
who, in my childhood, initiated me into a world of
fairies, pixies, and witches.

CONTENTS

RAISE HIGH THE CELTIC CURTAIN viii

PART 1:
MISCHIEF MAKERS AND MONSTROUS FAKERS
1

PART 2:
FOR LOVE ALONE
35

WHIPPETY STOURIE: WHAT THE GREEN FAIRY WANTS

Scotland
3

THOMAS THE RHYMER

Scotland
37

THE BROWNIE OF FERNE DEN (FERN GLEN) OR THE NOT SO BEASTLY BROWNIE

Scotland
9

THE WITCH OF LOCH ISLE (LAKE ISLAND)

Brittany
43

THE TOUCH OF DIRT (A TOUCH OF CLAY)

Wales
51

KATHERINE CRACKERNUTS: THE FAIRIES AND KATE CRACKERNUTS

Scotland
15

OISIN AND NIAMH

Ireland
57

THE HORNED WOMEN

Ireland
23

LA ROSE

Brittany
63

THE PÚCA AND THE PIPER

Ireland
29

PART 3:
LANDSCAPES IN CELTIC FOLKLORE
69

THE SEAL CATCHER AND THE SELKIE
Scotland
71

SEVEN YEARS IN MERLIN'S CRAIG
Scotland
77

FERGUS O'MARA'S ENCOUNTER WITH THE BARROW IMP
Ireland
83

SNORRO OF THE DWARF STONE AND THE TWO EARLS
Scotland
89

THE GIANT'S CAUSEWAY
Ireland
95

PART 4:
INTO THE WIDE AND WILD WORLD
101

THE RED ETIN
Scotland
103

THE DRAIGLIN HOGNEY
Scotland
111

ELIDOR IN THE KINGDOM OF THE LITTLE PEOPLE
Wales
117

LUGH
Ireland
123

CORMAC AND MANANNAN
Ireland
129

GLOSSARY 136
RESOURCES 139
REFERENCES 140
INDEX 141

RAISE HIGH THE CELTIC CURTAIN

Welcome to the extraordinary landscape of Celtic myth, legend, and folklore. Here, you will find tales of a bygone era when humans often encountered fairies, giants, and witches. The Celts lived in a mythical land located within the islands and territories of Western Europe, at the edge of the known world where anything was possible. There, waters, caves, and hillsides were filled with reclusive leprechauns, sly *selkies*, and helpful *brownies*.

The Celts preserved their myths through an oral tradition, passing down stories from one generation to the next, often reciting them around the bonfire. The guardians of these tales were bards and druids—a group of performers and teachers not unlike the wise figure of Merlin in Arthurian legends. Celtic leaders were known for their supernatural ability to see the future, understand the language of birds, cast spells of enchantment, and know the magic of the unseen otherworld.

But what can we learn from these ballads in our own busy world? In the story of the seal catcher and the selkie, you will discover that things are not always as they appear. The story of Thomas the Rhymer takes us deeper into the land of the elves, revealing how thoroughly a journey can transform us. Meanwhile, the tale of the green fairy shows how we can rely on our ingenuity and resourcefulness to overcome insurmountable odds. You will find something to take away from every myth and questions to help you think about each one.

These legends preserve the values of people who lived close to the supernatural realm of the *fae* and respected the power of nature. To live in these countries was to be caught up in the world of the *sidhe*. The druids kept their stories for thousands of years. Just as they passed down their oral tradition, these pages will pass these stories down to you.

Take this journey with me into unlocking some of the spellbinding secrets of the Celts.

MISCHIEF MAKERS
and
MONSTROUS FAKERS

Humans haven't always had the best relationship with fairies, who can be quite mischievous and cause all manner of trouble. Nevertheless, there are still lessons that can be learned from them.

Even the most unlikely creature might surprise you. So hold on to your britches as we meet some of these tricksters.

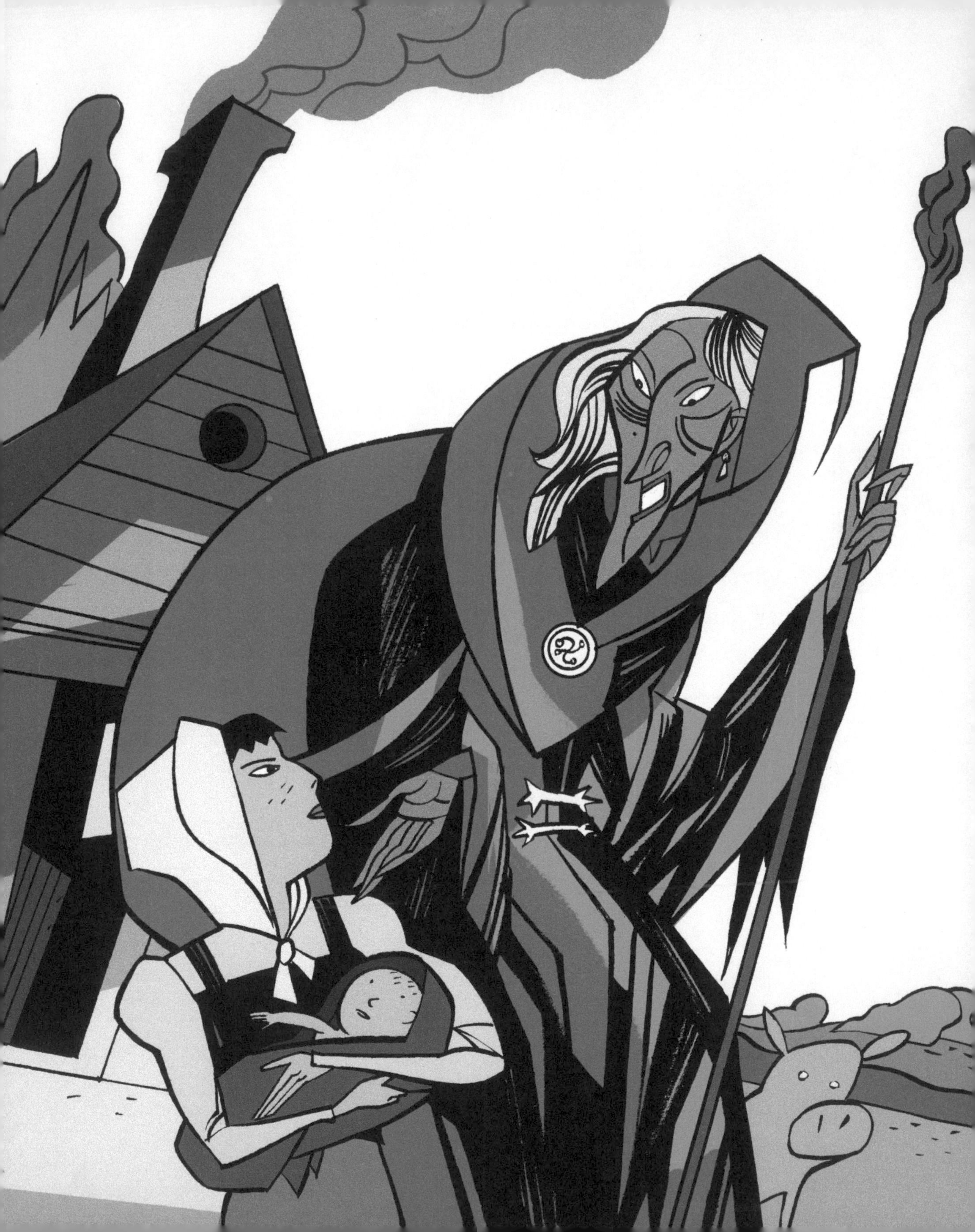

WHIPPETY STOURIE

WHAT THE GREEN FAIRY WANTS

Scotland

Long ago in the small village of Kittlerumpit, there lived a happy husband and wife. But their marriage was not to last. One day, the husband left his wife and was never heard from again. Some in the town thought he had enlisted in the navy and set out to sea, while others believed that he had been forced to join the army, but whatever the reason for his disappearance, he had left his wife and son in poverty.

The good woman had little means of caring for herself and the baby, and though her fellow villagers pitied her, no one came to her aid. She became so poor that she sold her belongings one by one, until all she had left was a pig about to give birth to a litter of baby piglets she hoped to sell.

One day, the good woman went to fill the pig's trough, yet found her sow lying on the ground, very ill and groaning in pain. *Surely this can't be happening*, thought the good woman. What would become of her with nothing left to sell? It was too much to think about, and she began to feel ill herself. She sat down next to the knocking stone and began to weep.

Wiping the tears from her eyes, she glanced toward the vast evergreen forest behind her house. To her surprise, she saw what appeared to be an elderly woman walking up the crooked path. Despite her age, this stately woman wore a long flowing gown woven of forest-green fabric, a crisp white apron, and an emerald-colored velvet cloak around her shoulders.

As the green-clad visitor approached, the good woman picked up her baby son from his basket. Even cradling her son, she couldn't hold back her sorrow and cried to the visitor, "I am the most unfortunate woman alive."

The visitor grimaced and said, "I do not wish to hear of your misfortune, about your ills, how your husband left you, and your poverty. Your pig is on the verge of death. But what will you give me if I heal your sick sow?"

Without thinking, the good woman replied, "I don't know what I can offer you, madam. I will give you anything in my possession."

Hearing that, the old woman was quick to seal the agreement. "Let's wet thumbs to that arrangement," she said, for wetting thumbs meant the agreement could never be broken.

Both women placed their thumbs under their own tongues and then hooked them together in a primitive handshake. No sooner had they made the arrangement than the old woman went into the pigsty and began muttering to the pig. Was she reciting some magic spell?

She took a small ointment jar from her pocket and rubbed it on the pig's snout, ears, and tail. The sow immediately rose, squealed with joy, and ran to her trough, where she began eating with a hearty appetite. The good woman couldn't believe her eyes and thanked the old woman for her help.

The old woman's reply was swift and chilled the good woman deep in her bones. "Now that I have healed your pig, I would like to collect on the debt owed to me. Give me your baby boy." The good woman was horrified by the cost of her shortsightedness and realized that the old woman was not a woman at all, but an evil fairy. The good woman pleaded for another option, but everything she offered was refused.

Yet even fairies must live by certain laws. As the green fairy said, "By fairy law I cannot take your child until three days have passed. If, at that time, you can guess my true name, your child will be spared." With that, the green fairy disappeared into the woods.

The good woman was distraught, consumed by the fear of losing her beloved son. She had to think of some way to outwit the green fairy. She decided to go for a walk to clear her thoughts. Not knowing where her feet were taking her, she walked into the woods behind her house.

In the middle of the forest sat an old quarry hole where people had once mined granite. Nearby, the good woman heard the sound of singing and the creaking of an ancient spinning wheel. Silently, she crept closer to the noise and—lo and behold!—saw the green fairy singing as she worked her wheel. The words she sang were clear and enchanting, meant for none to hear:

> "Little know our good dame
> at hame ('Little knows the good woman at home')
> That Whippety Stourie
> is my name."

The good woman was overjoyed, for she now knew the name of the green fairy. Her heart felt lighter knowing that she would be able to keep her child as she crept out of the forest. Now she thought about how to get even with the green fairy over the wicked distress she had caused, and decided to have some fun with her.

On the third day, the good woman placed her baby son beside the knocking stone and waited. As soon as she saw the fairy approach, she sat on the knocking stone and pretended to weep as the fairy said, "Good woman of Kittlerumpit, you know that I have come to collect on your debt. Hand over your child now."

The good woman pleaded, "Oh, sweet fairy. Please take the sow instead of my son."

"I have not come for pork. Give me your child immediately!"

Now the good woman pretended to be completely distraught. "Take me in place of my son. I cannot live without him."

Yet the fairy replied, "I will only have your child. No substitute will suffice."

The good woman then stood and quickly bowed down to the fairy. "In truth, fair queen, I should have known that I was not fit to tie the shoes of Whippety Stourie," she said, letting the fairy's name slip from her lips. Whippety Stourie was enraged! She shot up and screamed, knowing that she had been beaten, as she ran down the hill, fleeing from the scene of her defeat.

The good woman was quite pleased with herself. A darkness lifted from the woods as if an invisible fog had departed. She laughed, knowing that she not only had saved her son but also now had a healthy sow who would soon give birth to piglets.

BEHIND THE HOGNEYS, HOUNDS, AND WITCHES— QUESTIONS TO THINK ABOUT

- Are all fairies good?
- Was it wise for the good woman to strike a bargain before knowing the real cost?
- Was it fate that allowed the good woman to discover the fairy's name?

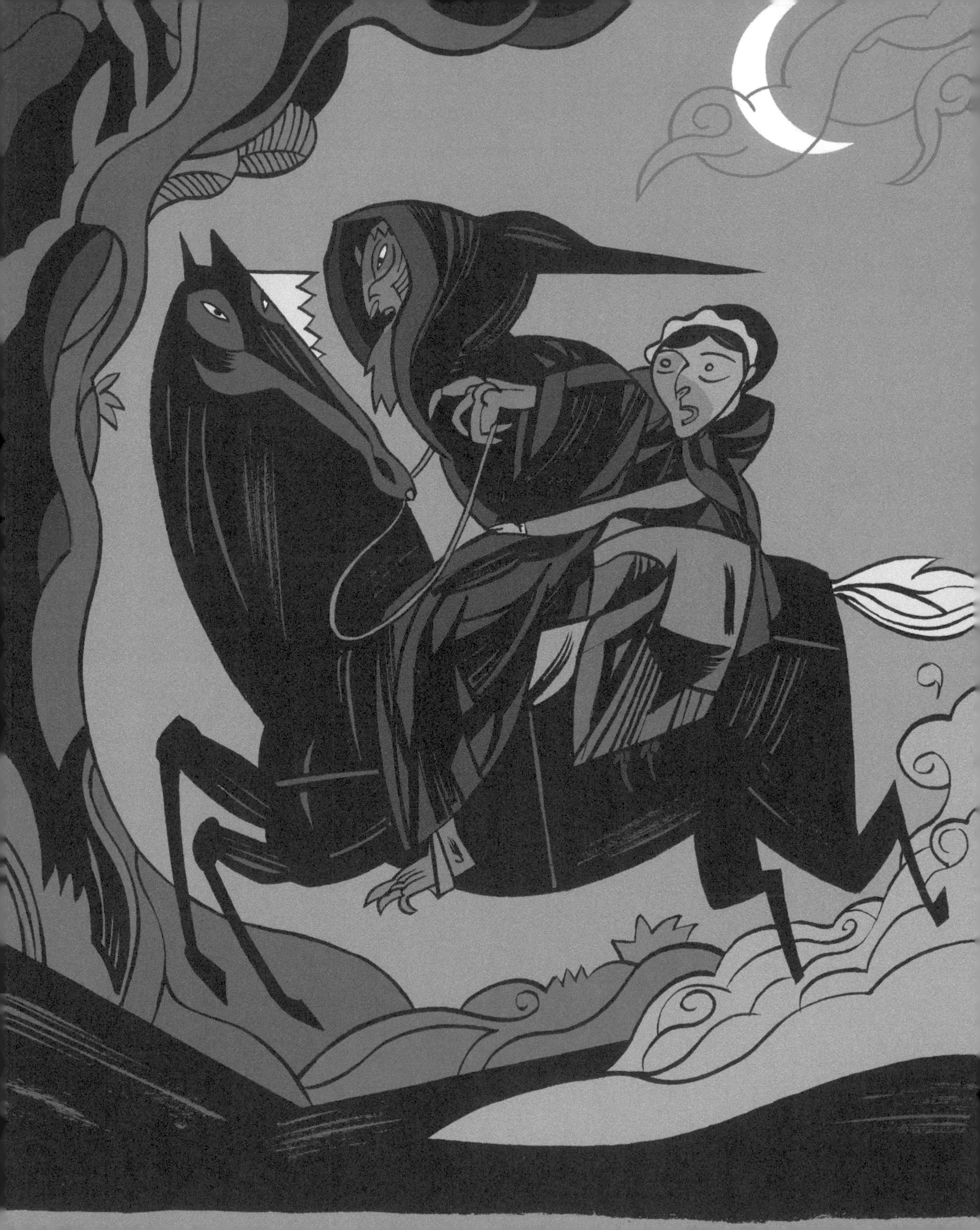

THE BROWNIE OF FERNE DEN

(FERN GLEN) OR THE NOT SO BEASTLY BROWNIE

Scotland

Hundreds of years ago, humans were much more aware of brownies, creatures who are not goblins or trolls, but who help those who keep their memories alive. This tale is the story of such a being.

In a valley deep in the heart of Scotland was a manor-farm called Ferne Den (Fern Glen), a place that took its name from the valley in which it sat. Those who wanted to come to the farm had to travel through this valley. Yet few people journeyed after nightfall, as scary stories were told about the brownie who lived there. Those who traveled at night reported seeing a dark figure lurking in the shadows, a sight that sent them running as fast as their feet and horses could carry them.

But the fearful villagers should have known better, for brownies don't intentionally scare humans. When treated respectfully, they are quite helpful to those who honor them, for brownies see themselves as guardians and custodians of farms, doing all manner of work but expecting nothing more than a simple supper and kindness in return. So it was in the old days that brownies would repair shoes, sow seeds, and harvest crops, accepting porridge with butter as payment for their good deeds.

Over time, people forgot the kind deeds of the brownies and only remembered their fear, but there was within this valley one woman who didn't fear the creature. The wife of the gentleman of Ferne Den was a gentle lady who respected the brownie, for she knew how hard he had worked while asking for no money in return. Therefore, she felt he was owed only the very best meal that she could furnish, and so it was that every evening she left out a bowl of porridge along with the most excellent milk and richest, thickest cream she could find.

Late one evening, the gentle lady became gravely ill. As her maid and butler watched her grow weaker by the hour, they felt great sadness at the possibility that she might perish. Without intervention from a healer, she would surely die. But since they feared encountering the brownie, no one was willing to travel to the next village and fetch the nurse, a renowned healer.

The gentleman of Ferne Den would have performed the errand himself, but he did not want to leave his sick wife. While the servants debated among themselves as to who would fetch the nurse, the brownie was watching from behind the kitchen door. Hidden in the shadow, he was a crooked and curious little man covered in hair with a long pointy beard, strangely long arms, and multicolored eyes. He stood not even six feet from the household staff but was unnoticed as he listened to their talk.

As was his evening custom, the brownie had walked up from his home deep in the glen, coming to the farmhouse to see if any work needed doing and, if so, to take his evening meal. Upon his arrival, however, he noticed that something was wrong, for when he usually arrived at the farm, only a single candlestick would be lit and everyone would be asleep. Tonight, the farm was bright with a flurry of activity.

He was saddened to discover that the mistress of the house had fallen ill, and furious to hear that the servants were so fearful of him, they refused to retrieve the nurse. He stomped his feet and muttered, "By my troth (truth), if they continue like this, the bonny lass will surely perish. Such foolishness. If they only knew how much I try to avoid them. They have nothing to fear from me." He decided to fetch the nurse himself.

The brownie pulled on the brawny farmer's long dark cloak that sat by the door, covering his oddly shaped body. He hoped that he could retrieve the nurse without raising suspicion, and so he ran to the stable and mounted the quickest horse. He whispered into its ear, "Travel quickly, my dear stallion. Gallop now!" It was as if the horse understood the brownie, for it pricked up its ears, let out a neigh, and galloped as fast as the wind, speeding down the path leading through the shadowy glen.

He arrived at the nurse's cottage in a flash, but the hour was late and the nurse fast asleep. Quickly, the brownie approached her window and tapped on it frantically to wake the old nurse. Sensing the urgency in the rapping, she shot out of bed and threw open the window without putting on her spectacles. Before she could ask what the commotion was about, the brownie made his request.

"Good woman, you must come with me now, for the fair lady of Ferne Den is gravely ill."

"Have they sent a cart to fetch me?"

"Please, make haste and climb into the saddle behind me. I swear I will get you to the farm safely."

The brownie's voice was confident and strong, and so she quickly dressed, packed her bag of medicines, and mounted the horse. She wrapped her arms around the stranger's curiously small waist. Hardly a word was spoken between them until they approached the foreboding glen. The nurse began to feel uneasy, and as the shadows crept in around them, her courage left her.

Quietly she asked the stranger, "Do you think we shall see the brownie tonight? I fear to look on such a creature, for folks speak all manner of odd stories about him."

He let out a full-bellied laugh and said, "Fear not, dear woman. I promise that _I_ am the most fearsome creature you will encounter tonight."

"I shall not worry then, for even though I have not seen your face, the care you show for the fair lady tells me that you are of a fine and gentle character."

The unlikely pair fell back into silence as they traveled until they arrived at the farm. The brownie promptly slid off the horse and lowered the nurse to the ground. As he did so, his cloak tangled up and fell from his twisted body, revealing his true self.

"What in the world? What kind of man are you?" asked the nurse as the early morning light shone upon his gangly features. "What makes your eyes so large? And what of your feet? They hardly resemble those of a grown man."

The brownie laughed and said, "I have walked thousands of miles in my time without a horse. I hear that doing so makes feet quite unseemly. But waste no time talking to me, for the mistress of the house needs you. Go that way, and if anyone asks you how you came here so quickly, tell them that you rode behind the brownie of Ferne Den." The wise nurse then made her way into the manor house and told the family of her most fantastic journey.

BEHIND THE HOGNEYS, HOUNDS, AND WITCHES— QUESTIONS TO THINK ABOUT

- Is it fair to judge someone by how they appear?
- Are fears always rational, or are they sometimes unfounded?
- Have you ever received help from someone who you didn't expect to assist you?

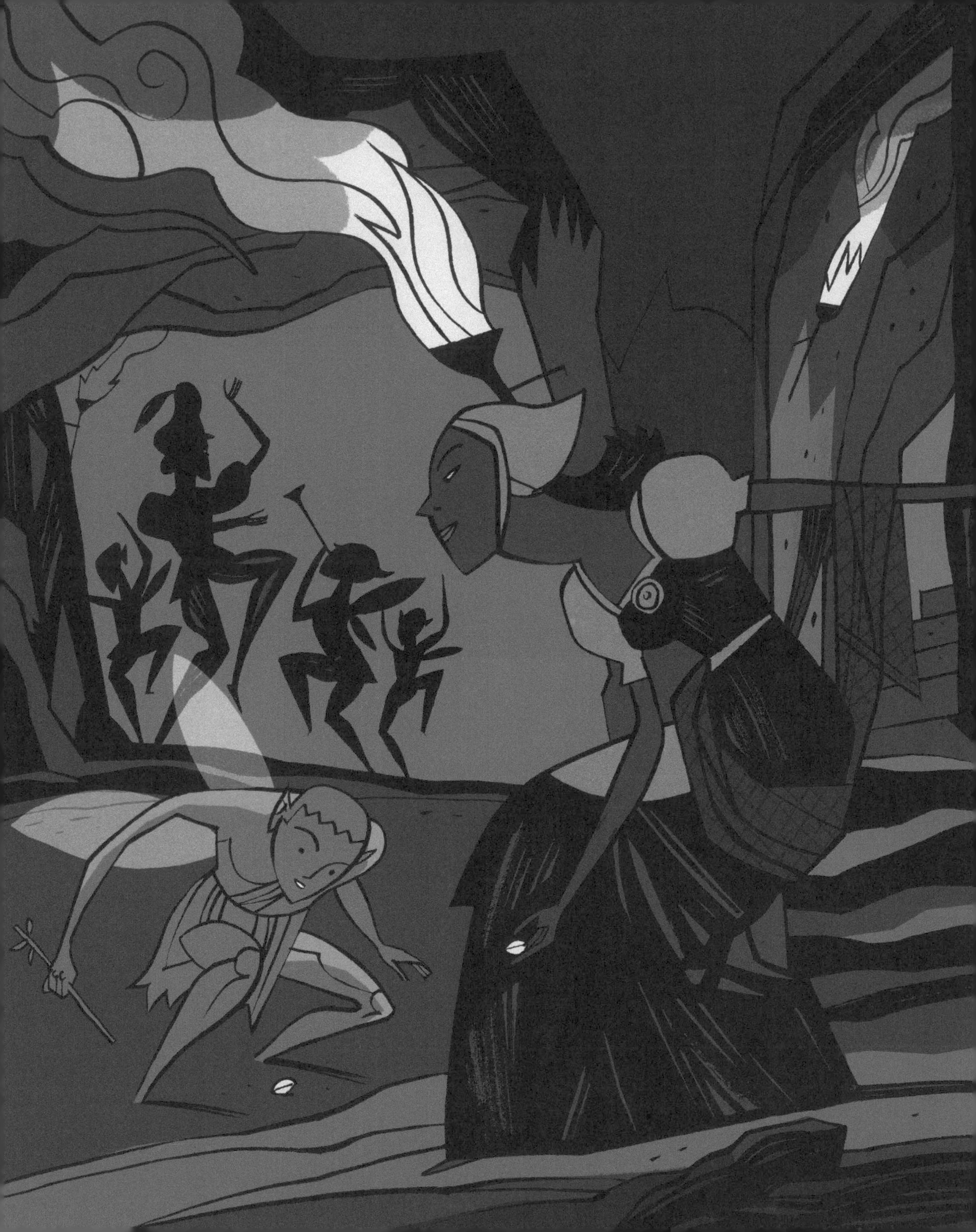

KATHERINE CRACKERNUTS

THE FAIRIES AND KATE CRACKERNUTS

Scotland

Once upon a time there was a beautiful and kind-hearted young princess named Velvet Cheeks. Her father, the king, loved her very much. However, he dearly wanted his daughter to have a sister to play with and a mother to love. His wife had passed away some years before, and the time had come for him to remarry.

After searching for a suitable wife, he decided to wed a countess who lived nearby, one who had a daughter named Katherine. Both Velvet Cheeks and Katherine were roughly the same age.

The union was beautiful, and the young princess became the best of friends with the countess's daughter. However, all was not well. The new queen was full of ambition and wanted her daughter—and only her daughter—to become queen. She knew that this was impossible as long as Princess Velvet Cheeks remained beautiful.

Among the servants was an old woman who tended hens and was said to be a witch. So, one evening in the darkness of night, the queen quietly crept down to the old woman's cottage to seek her help, and the door creaked loudly as it opened.

The old woman was, indeed, willing to help and said, "Send Velvet Cheeks to me tomorrow before she has eaten a bite of breakfast. My spell is a powerful one but will only work if she hasn't eaten even a morsel of food."

The next morning, the queen asked her stepdaughter to run down to the old woman who raised hens and fetch some eggs, saying she must do it before eating anything.

The princess was a good girl and agreed to fetch the eggs, yet her stomach ached with hunger. So Velvet Cheeks quickly ran to the pantry and ate a slice of cake before going to the old woman's cottage. She quickly scurried to the chicken coop and asked for eggs from the old woman, who replied, "Lift the lid off that corner pot, and you will find the eggs that you seek." The princess did so and placed the eggs in her own basket. The old woman said, "Go to your mother, lass, and tell her my advice is to keep the pantry door locked."

Although Velvet Cheeks didn't understand the message, the queen did, gathering that the young princess had foiled her plans by eating something before fetching the eggs.

The next morning, the queen once again asked her stepdaughter to fetch some eggs. This time, however, the queen locked the pantry door. So even though the princess was hungry and was suspicious of her stepmother's motives, she couldn't eat anything. On the way to the cottage, she plucked some snap peas growing on a vine and ate a few pods. The same thing occurred as had the previous day, so the princess was sent home to her stepmother with another message.

The queen was enraged. How had the princess bested her again? To ensure that the princess did not outwit her the next day, the queen accompanied her to make sure that Velvet Cheeks didn't eat anything.

When they arrived at the old woman's cottage, the princess did precisely as she had done before, lifting the lid off the pot and removing the eggs. To her astonishment, her head fell off and was replaced by the head of a bleating sheep.

The cruel queen laughed at this wicked spell, for no prince would want to marry Velvet Cheeks now.

The princess ran home with her head covered by a basket, weeping the entire way. Princess Katherine loved Velvet Cheeks very much and was furious when she discovered what her mother had done. To escape the wicked queen, Katherine led her sister out of the castle that night to seek a cure for the curse.

They walked all night and all the next day and eventually reached a splendid palace. Princess Katherine told Velvet Cheeks of her plan to find work so they could live a comfortable life. But Velvet Cheeks was ashamed and said, "They will not hire you if they know you have a sister who has the head of a sheep." But Katherine had a plan.

"Keep a shawl around your head and leave the rest to me."

Katherine knocked on the palace door and asked if there was any work to be had. Sure enough, there was a job for hire. However, the serving woman asked why Velvet Cheeks had her head wrapped up in such an odd manner.

"My sister has long been troubled by beastly headaches," said Katherine, "and wears the shawl over her head to muffle loud noises."

By chance, the crown prince of the palace was equally sick with a strange illness. He was quite restless at night and needed someone to stay by him at all times. The king was skeptical at first, but was won over by Katherine's calm nature, and so he hired the young lass to watch over the sickly prince.

All evening she watched over him, but nothing remarkable happened until just after midnight. As she started drifting off to sleep, Katherine awoke to the sound of the prince dressing and running downstairs. She quickly followed, chasing him into the courtyard only to see him mount a horse.

Katherine thought to herself, *I must follow him, for I fear he is bewitched.* Silently she mounted another horse and followed the prince. As they rode off, she grabbed a handful of nuts from an overhanging hazelnut tree, as she didn't know when she might next eat.

They rode many miles, pausing just before a grand mound. The prince seemed possessed, and Katherine heard him whisper something quick and hushed. The hill appeared to respond to the prince's words, for a large cavern opened up in front of them. The horse galloped ahead fearlessly, and as if by magic, torches were set aflame within the cave as they passed. The flickering light revealed that this was no ordinary cavern, but a great hall set with sconces and filled with elaborately set tables at which sat fairies.

When the fairies saw the young prince, they ran to him and frolicked and danced. The sprites were so preoccupied with dancing that no one noticed Katherine. She silently made her way over to what appeared to be a young child lying on the ground playing with a wand, strangely drawn toward the lad, feeling that he was of some importance.

The fairies continued to dance and sing. As the dancers passed, Katherine heard them sing about a golden wand that could cure enchantments. That gave Katherine an idea. Could the wand the fairies were singing about be the one in the young boy's hand? There was only one way to find out.

She reached into her pocket, pulled out some nuts, and rolled them toward the child. As if enchanted by the nuts, the boy dropped the wand and reached toward them. Hastily, Katherine picked up the golden wand, hid it under her apron, and crept away. The lad must have been ravenous, as he so diligently went about cracking the nuts that he didn't notice his wand had gone missing.

Soon, the sun's rays started peeking into the cave, and all in a hurry the dancing prince readied himself to leave. The fairies scurried back into their hiding places, and Katherine silently slid into her horse's saddle. In a flash, both horses rode from the cavern back to the castle.

Arriving at the palace, Katherine ran to her stepsister, touching her three times with the golden wand. Lo and behold, the sheep's head popped off Velvet Cheeks's neck, and her own head miraculously returned.

In the morning, the king asked Katherine how the prince had fared through the night. She advised him that his son was well but she felt that if given another night she might be able to cure him. The king thought the young woman must surely be a healer, as he had heard of how she had cured her sister of her illness, and he agreed.

At midnight, the prince rose again, and both he and Katherine journeyed to the fairy mound. All manner of elf and sprite danced inside as Katherine sat upon a stone and waited. The fairies sang enchanted lyrics about taking away the cares of the prince. All the while, Katherine was looking for the young boy. Her instinct suggested he might hold the cure to the prince's illness.

After some time, the young boy could be seen playing with a little cookie shaped like a bird. Katherine could hear the boy talk to the bird-shaped cookie, and she crept closer to listen. As she neared, she heard him say in a singsong voice, "Three bites from this bird will heal a prince of his illness."

She removed nuts from her pocket once again and rolled them toward the little boy. He dropped the bird cookie and picked up the nuts. Katherine quickly grabbed the cookie and hid it beneath her apron.

Time passed, yet in what seemed like a few minutes, dawn approached, and the sprites retreated to their hiding places. Katherine and the prince each left on horseback and rode to the castle. Still under the enchantment, the prince went up to his room. Katherine followed. Soon he shook his head in the manner that a horse might, and the spell released him.

Katherine went to the prince and said, "I brought you a snack. I hope you like cookies." Like most people, the prince did, indeed, like cookies and began eating the one on his tray. After taking one bite, his strength began to return. After two bites, his voice became stronger. With a third bite, color returned to his face and flushed his cheeks a bright pink. The prince was now as handsome as he had ever been and standing tall once again.

Soon the king entered the chambers to see if Katherine had, by chance, been able to improve his son's condition. What did he see but the young prince cracking nuts with Katherine! Some of the very same nuts Katherine had plucked from the hazelnut tree.

The king was so delighted that his son had been cured that he dubbed Katherine "Crackernuts." As the king could see that she and the prince were quite fond of each other, he asked if the two might want to get engaged, to which both happily agreed.

Quite surprisingly, the king's other son then entered with Velvet Cheeks, whom he had met the day before. The two were already profoundly fond of each other. And as many old tales end, "They all lived happily ever after."

BEHIND THE HOGNEYS, HOUNDS, AND WITCHES— QUESTIONS TO THINK ABOUT

- Is it fair for a stepparent to treat a stepchild differently?
- Just as with the sisters, can friends and siblings help us get through difficult times?
- Is it okay for a child to question an adult's motives if the child knows the adult is wrong?

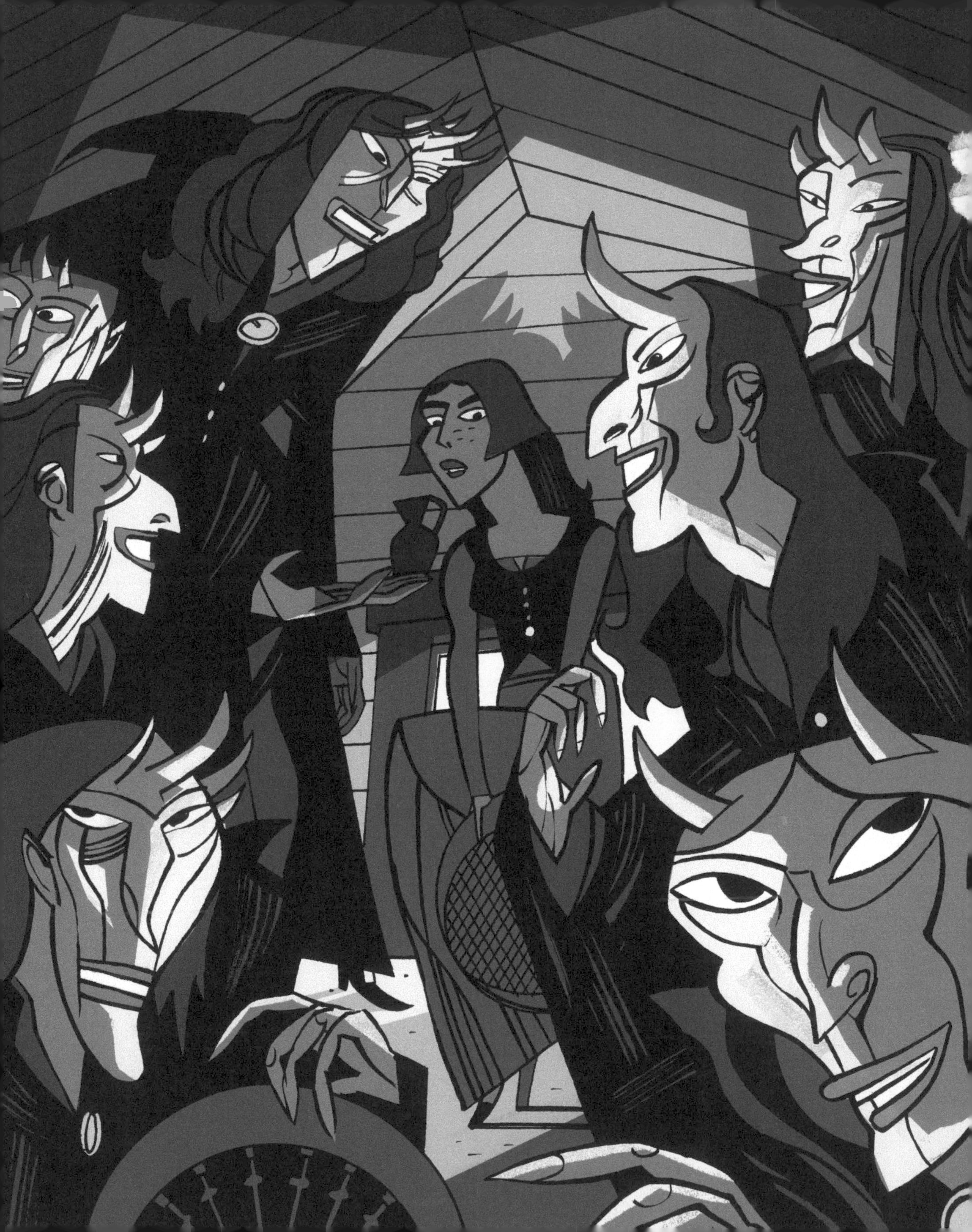

THE HORNED WOMEN

Ireland

Late one Halloween Eve, a noblewoman stayed up late to finish carding wool to get it ready for spinning. All the servants had gone to sleep, and the only sound that could be heard throughout the house was the soft scraping of wool.

The noblewoman had nearly finished her work when all of a sudden there was a loud knock at the door.

"Open the door! Open the door!" cried a harsh, demanding voice.

"Who's there?" inquired the noblewoman.

"Who do you think it is? I am the Witch of One Horn," the voice replied.

The noblewoman thought that it must be a joke, for no one had ever heard of a horned witch. Once she cracked the door open, a middle-aged woman pushed her way in, carrying a pair of wool carders in hand.

The noblewoman thought to herself, *Who would be so bold as to enter in such haste?* It was at that moment that she noticed a great horn right in the middle of the intruder's forehead.

Without speaking another word, the visitor sat down by the central hearth, where a massive fire flickered. She began to work feverishly on the wool at an unusually quick pace. Quite abruptly, she paused, asking the noblewoman, "Where are my sisters? They are late."

Soon there was another rapping at the door. Just as before, a voice called out, "Open the door! Open the door!"

At this point the noblewoman was not interested in any more midnight guests and did not answer. With a loud thud, the door flung open on its own, and a second witch entered. She had not one but two large horns on her forehead and carried a spinning wheel.

"Who are you?" asked the noblewoman.

"I am the Witch of Two Horns." And then with a dismissive wave she said, "Now leave me in peace, as I must spin." The Witch of Two Horns sat beside her sister and worked at an even more feverish pace than her single-horned sibling.

So it was that all night long there were repeated knocks, and with each knock another witch came in until, at last, there were twelve clustered around the hearth, each working away, and each with horns growing from their heads.

The witches worked in unison, each having a part to play in transforming the wool into a woven form. As they worked through the night, they sang an old tune that the noblewoman could not understand, but they spoke not a word directly to her.

The women were dreadful to look upon and odd to listen to as their words were ancient and foreign and their horned heads were frightful. Fearful, the noblewoman could not move and almost fainted. She tried to scream for help but found she could not speak.

One of the witches called to the noblewoman in Gaelic, a language she understood.

"Get to the kitchen and make us a cake!" Instantly, the noblewoman sprang to her feet. She could not seem to deny whatever the witches demanded. She searched high and low for a bucket with which to fetch some water to begin the cake's batter, but alas, she could not find one.

The witches laughed and called to the noblewoman, "Take a sieve and fetch the water."

The noblewoman knew quite well that a sieve would not hold water, but she did as she was told and tried to collect the water from the well. It was no use; the sieve simply would not hold water.

From the darkness of the well, a voice called out to her. "Take some moss and yellow clay. Bind them together and make plaster to seal the sieve. That should hold it, madam." The noblewoman looked around, but it was so dark that she could not find who had spoken. She did as the voice told, and the sieve now held water.

The voice then said, "Return to your home. Enter from the north and repeat this phrase: 'The Fenian women's mountain and the sky above it are ablaze with fire.'"

The noblewoman did exactly as she was instructed. Immediately upon saying the phrase, she heard wailing coming from the house. It sounded as if the witches were in great pain. They shrieked as they ran, fleeing in the direction of Slievenamon, a mountain known to be home to many witches. The spirit of the well advised the noblewoman to prepare for the witches' return with their enchantments and ill intent.

When the noblewoman reentered, she saw that the witches had made a cake in her absence, but a wicked one crafted with blood from members of her sleeping family. Thinking back to the stories that her mother had told her as a child, the noblewoman knew that such a creation could be used to break the powerful enchantment placed upon them, so she put a bite of cake in each of her children's mouths. The spell quickly lifted. She sprinkled the water she had used to bathe her children's feet across the threshold of the house. This, too, would break enchantments, many of which the witches might be intent on using. Lastly, she barred the front door with a large slab of wood to ensure that the witches could not enter.

True to the wisdom from the spirit of the well, the witches returned, and they were enraged. They shrieked and called forth all sorts of ill chants.

"Open the door! Open the door!" they screamed in furious and terrible voices.

"Open, feet-water!" they growled at the ground.

The foot-water replied, "I cannot, as I am all scattered on the ground, and I now trickle down to the lake."

"Open the door! Open the door! Open this door, wood, and henge."

"I cannot," replied the door, "for I am blocked by a beam and have no power to move at all."

"Open the door! Open the door! Open this door, the cake that we mingled with blood and flour."

But the witches' cries were in vain as the cake solemnly replied, "I cannot open the door, as I am crumbled and bruised, and my blood now rests upon the lips of those you stole it from."

The witches then realized they had been defeated. They shrieked and flew through the air on their besoms (brooms), cursing the spirit of the well, for they knew none other that could have helped the noblewoman.

At last it was dawn, and the noblewoman now had peace. She surveyed the yard and discovered that one of the witches had lost her cloak. The noblewoman kept it as a token of that night's unbelievable encounter and her victory over the witches.

BEHIND THE HOGNEYS, HOUNDS, AND WITCHES— QUESTIONS TO THINK ABOUT

- Is there a reason that the noblewoman shouldn't have opened the door to strangers?
- Do you know of some other ways that the noblewoman could have defeated the witches?
- The spirit of the well helped the lady defeat the witches. Do you know other helpers who could help you if you are in trouble?

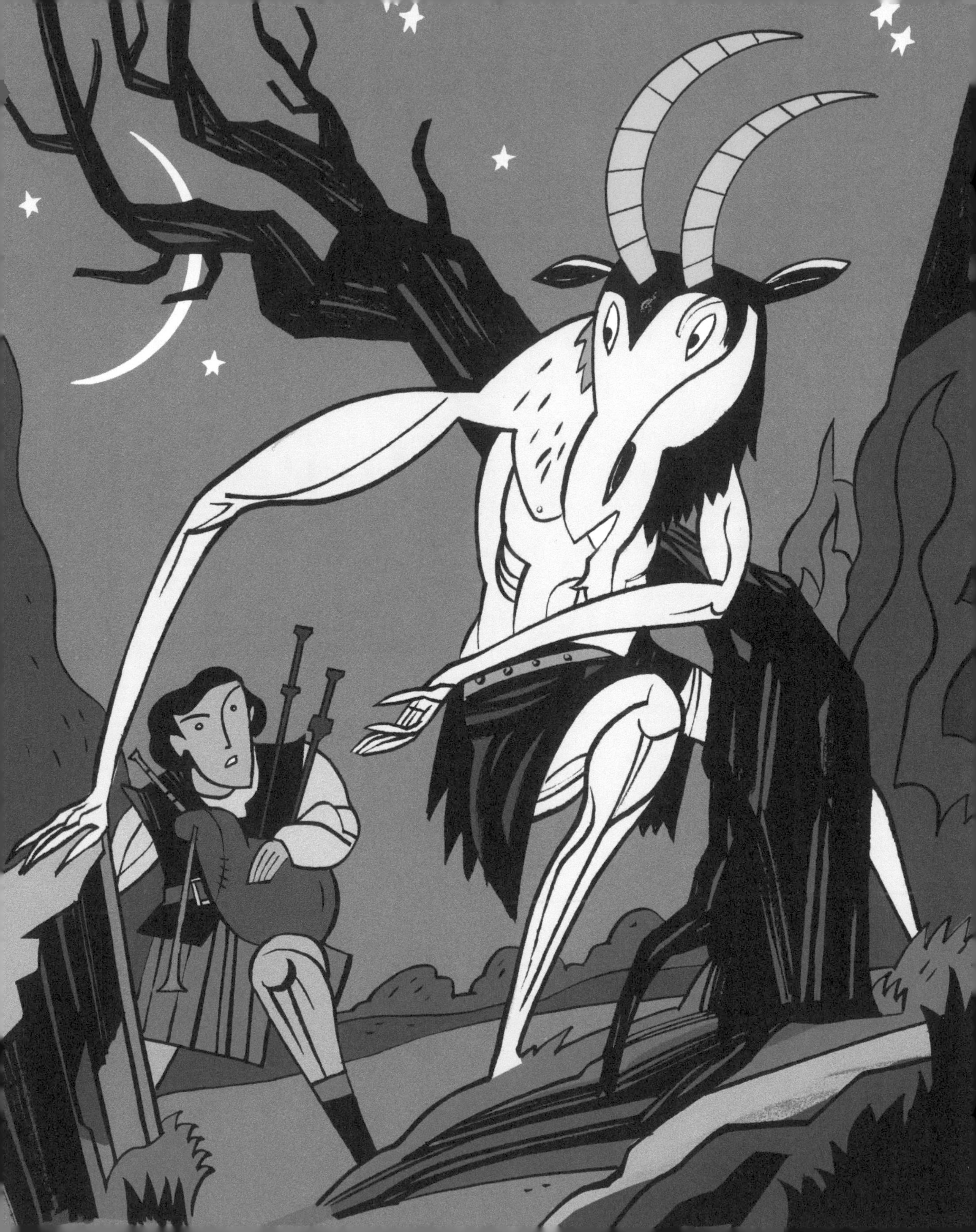

THE PÚCA AND THE PIPER

Ireland

In the faraway county of Galway in the kingdom of Northern Ireland, there lived a man known for his excessive love of music. Even though he enjoyed playing his bagpipe, he only knew one tune; that song is known as the "Black Rogue."

Knowing the piper could only play a single song, the local men liked to play a trick on the man, paying him for his services but laughing when they asked him to play a song he didn't know. The piper was a good man, even if he was known for once having stolen the priest's goose.

There came a night when the piper had a lot of ale, and he walked along the country road stumbling this way and that for hours before he reached the bridge near his mother's home.

The piper decided to take a break from his long walk and began to play the only song he knew, as a *púca* snuck up behind him. Now púcas are exotic creatures with the horns of a goat and the body of a large man. Intent on having some fun with the piper, the púca snatched up the man and flung him over his back, not unlike a backpack.

The piper grabbed the creature's horns and pummeled his back. "Let me go, you foul creature, or may you be forever cursed! I need to give my mother money for the market. Let me go on my way."

"Don't worry about your mother, lad," said the púca, "Hold on to my horns tightly because if you fall you will surely perish." The piper looked down, and, sure enough, he was hanging off the bridge. He grabbed even more tightly to the creature's horns.

The púca slowly lifted him from the edge of the bridge and placed him safely on the ground. Then the creature said, "Play for me the tune called 'Shan Van Vocht.'"

"I'm sorry, but I don't know that song," said the piper.

"It doesn't matter if you know the song or not," replied the púca. "Begin to play and I will enchant you so that you know it."

The piper blew into the bag of his pipes and began to play. It was a surprise when he discovered that not only did he know the tune, but a fairer rendition of the song had never been played.

"Mark my word! This is amazing!" exclaimed the piper. "But where are you taking me?"

"Tonight, there is an enormous feast in the abode of the *banshee*," said the púca. "The house sits right atop Croagh Patrick, and I am taking you there so that you can play the finest music for us. You will be handsomely rewarded for your trouble."

The piper replied, "What a coincidence. I was to go to Croagh Patrick on a pilgrimage as penance for stealing a goose from Father William."

The púca carried the man across the countryside, tramping though hills, swampland, and forest, until they reached their destination— the shadowy Croagh Patrick.

The púca stomped three times on the mountainside. In response, a large door opened into the very bowels of the hill. Inside was a great hall with magnificent finery. In the middle of the grand room sat a massive golden table with hundreds of elderly women around it. They rose in unison and said, "Púca of November, we welcome you to our autumn gathering. But who is this human who you have brought with you?"

The púca replied, "He is the best piper in all the land."

At the end of the table, the eldest women stood and picked up her staff. She struck the floor forcefully with it, and a door opened at the side of the cavern. When the piper looked over, he saw none other than Father William's white goose alive and well—the very same one he had stolen at last St. Martin's Mass.

"Bless my soul," said the piper. "My mother and I ate that very goose. All but a single wing, which I gave to a woman named Mary. It was she who told the priest of my deed." This was a magical goose that the fairies had created to taunt him.

The goose cleared the table of all of the dirty dishes. Then the púca said, "Play music for these fairy women, good sir."

The piper began to play as the women danced around the grand hall, kicking up their feet and cheering. They danced all evening until their feet hurt. The púca then requested that the women pay the piper for his services, and all obliged, giving him one gold piece each.

In astonishment, the piper said, "I can hardly believe it. I am as rich as a prince."

Now that the evening's festivities had come to a close, the púca said, "Piper, come with me, and I will bring you back home."

As they were leaving, the goose gave the piper a new set of bagpipes as the fairy women had told it to do. The piper thanked the goose and quickly climbed atop the púca. They left, traveling as fast as a crow can fly. It was not long before they reached their destination, and the púca urged the piper to go home.

"You have been given good sense and the gift of music. Use them wisely," he warned, and in a flash, the púca vanished. Soon the piper was at his mother's house. He knocked and said, "Let me in, Mother, for I am now as rich as a prince!"

From inside he heard laughter, "Boy, you must have been dreaming! There is no possible way that you could be rich."

"I did not dream," said the piper. "I haven't slept even a wink."

His mother opened the door, and he gave her all the money he had been paid that night. "Now wait until you hear me play the pipes," he said.

As he worked the pipes, an awful sound came forth, the sound of a thousand geese, as if all the flocks of Ireland were calling out together. It was a dreadful noise and even woke his neighbors, who laughed at him. That was until he brought out his old pipes, the ones he used before the goose's gift, and played gorgeous music the likes of which had never been heard in that county. It was then that he told them everything that had happened that night.

Soon everyone went to bed, and when the man's mother woke up the next morning, she went to count the money her son had earned but instead of gold coins found only leaves.

Seeing this, the piper decided that he should go confess to the priest all that had happened. Father William, however, did not believe him— at least not until the piper played the new pipes and the priest heard the honking sound of geese.

"Bless my soul," the priest exclaimed, before the piper played the old pipes beautifully, and the priest knew that his story was true. From that day forward, the piper was known as the best piper in all of Ireland.

BEHIND THE HOGNEYS, HOUNDS, AND WITCHES— QUESTIONS TO THINK ABOUT

- Was the púca a human, or was he an animal?
- Even though the púca gave gifts to the piper, was it wrong of him to kidnap him?
- Why didn't the townsfolk believe the piper? Was it because he was a thief?
- Should the piper have served his punishment earlier for stealing the goose?

FOR LOVE ALONE

Even during the heroic age of the early Celts, love was a force to be reckoned with. Love could tame the most ferocious warrior and bring one through challenges in order to save someone they treasured. In the story of the Witch of Loch Isle (Lake Island), you will learn how heroines performed great feats to save their loved ones. In the story of La Rose, you will come to understand that sometimes love can be found in the most unexpected of places.

Join me on the next stage of our adventure.

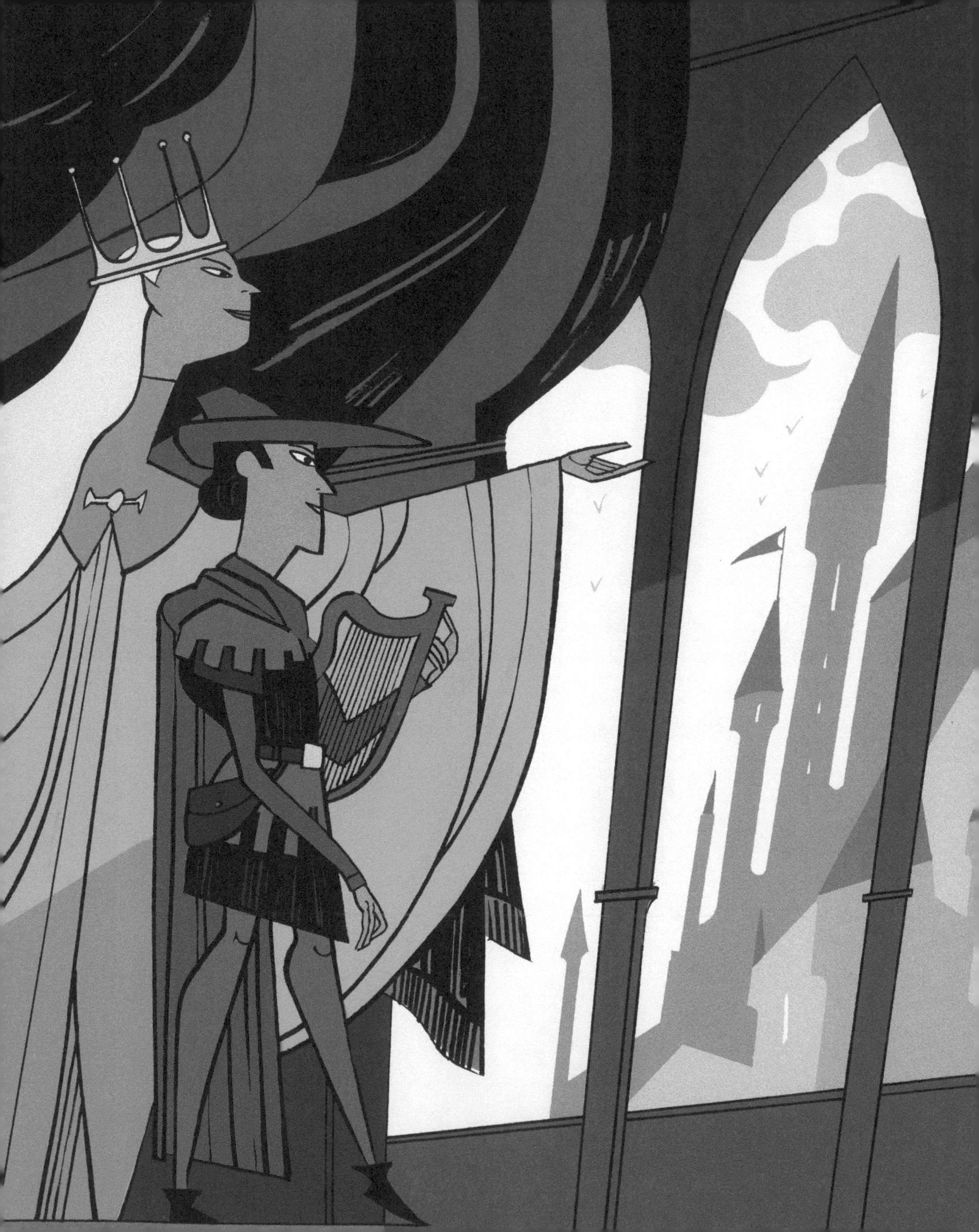

THOMAS THE RHYMER

Scotland

Long ago in Earlston, Scotland, there lived a man by the name of Thomas. He was a gentle fellow and a bard by profession. Bards did a great many things, giving speeches to the king's court, preserving history, and creating great works of poetry. Because of his talents, this man became known as Thomas the Rhymer.

One evening, Thomas was taking an evening stroll along the riverbank. He gazed at the water, enjoying the hums, chirps, and sounds of nature. Often, he would get lost in a daze. But today he was startled by the sound of loud thumping hooves and turned to see an elf woman riding toward him on a large white horse. This steed was ivory as bone—clearly otherworldly—and brilliant silver bells dangled from its mane. They jingled as the stallion trotted down the path.

Thomas was struck by the elf woman's appearance, so radiant was she that he thought she must be the Queen of Heaven, wearing a beautifully woven green dress. The elf woman snorted down at him as Thomas exclaimed, "Hail, great Queen of Heaven! Never before have I seen a woman as stunning as you!"

The unearthly woman dismounted her horse, and as she approached, she laughed aloud, "Thomas! You have called me wrongly. I am not the Queen of Heaven but the Queen of the Elves!"

Surely his mother had told him stories about the elves, but he had never believed them. He began to consider the possibility that he was dreaming, so he pinched himself. He felt the sharp pain immediately. "Why have you come to see me, great Queen?"

The elf queen replied, "I bid you come with me to Alfheim. Serve me there for seven years. If you do, you will be handsomely rewarded."

The elf queen was charming, and her gaze enchanted Thomas, and so he followed as she mounted her steed and rode back to her homeland. They traveled over great distances, crossing a wide rushing river and mountains and passing through shaded dales. Eventually, they stopped to rest in a vast desert in the middle of nowhere, a desolate country where Thomas could see nothing but emptiness.

Once the horse had rested, the elf queen and Thomas began to ride once again.

The elf queen turned to Thomas and said, "I shall now show you three wonders." She pointed to the east. "Do you see that narrow road covered in thornbushes? That is the path to heaven."

Then she pointed to the south. "Look at the roadway before you. It is the path of wickedness that leads to the underworld—a horrible place. Lastly, you have the third road in front of you. It twists and turns through the hills to the west. That is our path—the road to Alfheim."

The pair continued on their journey. Thomas and the queen rode the horse day and night. Nighttime was odd in this land because there were no stars or moon. Without any stars in the sky to give an idea of time, Thomas had no idea how long they had been traveling, but eventually he saw a distant glow on the horizon. It grew brighter and brighter until Thomas was finally able to take in the land all around him.

It was the lushest, most beautiful area he had ever seen, with enormous mountains and vast forests. The horse came to rest in a sprawling orchard, and Thomas and the elf queen dismounted. The queen went to one of the trees, plucked an apple, and handed it to Thomas.

"Thomas," she said, "this is your reward for following me. Once you eat it, you will have the power of prophecy." Thomas promptly began nibbling at the apple, much the way a squirrel eats a nut, and followed the queen into her magnificent castle. It was larger than any he had ever known, and the spires reached toward the sky.

Once they were inside, the queen's servants gave Thomas clothes of green silk and shoes of the softest fern-colored velvet.

He settled into his new life in the elf kingdom, and Thomas proudly served the queen and was immensely happy. Time passed quickly, and as if he had been under a spell, seven years passed in what seemed like seven hours.

The queen allowed Thomas to leave her castle and return home, as he needed to check on his mother and family. His return took many days of travel, but soon Thomas noticed the landscape changing. He was back in his homeland.

Once home, Thomas resumed his work as a bard. He journeyed from kingdom to kingdom, creating poetry for royalty and sharing prophecies thanks to his newfound insight. Much like other bards of his era, Thomas became famous for his ability to see the future. He gained the name "Thomas the True" and was renowned through-out Scotland. For many years, Thomas faithfully served kings and lords, but he grew tired of the mortal world. He missed the sites he'd seen in the realm of the elves and everything about it, but mostly he missed the queen.

So it was that one day, the queen returned, telling Thomas that she could take him back to Alfheim if he so desired. He thought long and hard about his choice. He loved Scotland, his first true home, but it no longer was the country he once knew. It had changed so much that it no longer felt the same to him.

Thomas prepared for his journey and went to each of his friends' houses, embraced his friends tightly one last time, and wished them well. He then mounted the queen's horse, and they departed. Several riders followed them, but as soon as they turned a bend, Thomas and the queen disappeared from view.

Legend has it that even though 750 years have passed since that time, Thomas still lives in Alfheim. They say that he returns to Scotland every summer's eve, accompanied by the elf riders and sprites who visit to play mischievous games. Some say that Thomas appears as an old man, while others say that he is energetic, eternally youthful, and ageless.

BEHIND THE HOGNEYS, HOUNDS, AND WITCHES— QUESTIONS TO THINK ABOUT

- How did Thomas's adventure change him?
- How do elves differ from humans?
- How are elves and humans the same?
- Why did the elf queen take Thomas to Alfheim?

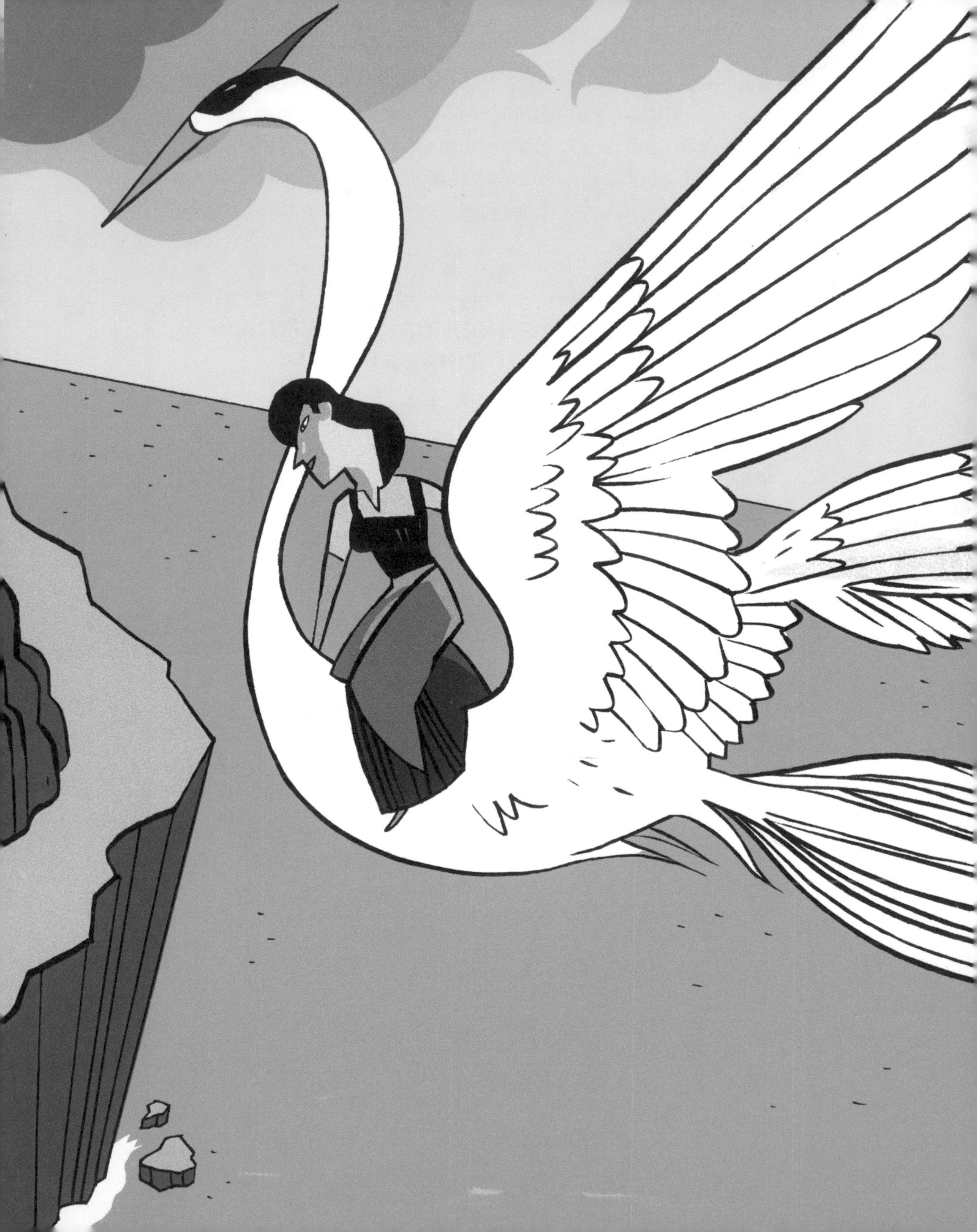

THE WITCH OF LOCH ISLE

(LAKE ISLAND)

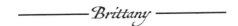
Brittany

In rural France in the province of Brittany was a small town by the name of Lannilis, and there lived two youths, Houarn and Bella, who were in love.

They were orphans serving a land baron and didn't have much except their strong and faithful love for each other. Even so, they longed for more than their meager life.

"I wish I had money to buy a cow and pig," said Houarn. "I would purchase some land, and we could get married."

"I would love that," replied Bella and sighed. "But, Houarn, we are most unlucky."

Their complaints piled up, and finally Houarn decided that he could no longer wait for their fortunes to change. He had to act. He told Bella of his plans to leave town on a quest to seek out riches he was sure were due him.

Bella objected to Houarn's plans, but it was to no avail, for Houarn had made up his mind.

"I am doing this for both of us, Bella. If I find my fortune, we can get married."

Bella had no choice but to give in, but she had some magic up her sleeve. "If you must go, go with my blessing. But I want to give you a token of my goodwill. Wait for me."

She ran home, went to her closet, and pulled out three enchanted items left to her by her parents: a bell on a length of ribbon, a knife, and a stick. She placed the ribbon holding the bell over Houarn's head and handed him the knife, telling him, "These will help when you are in need. I will keep the stick so that I may find you if you are in trouble."

The couple kissed goodbye, and Houarn placed the items deep in his knapsack. He traveled until he found himself in Pont-Aven, a tiny village three days south of Lannilis. It was a quaint town, and Houarn decided to stay for a couple of days.

One morning, Houarn overheard two traders sharing stories about a witch who lived not far away on a local island named for the lake inside it. This witch, the traders said, was richer than all the kings in the entire world combined, and even her furniture was made of solid gold. The traders sang praises of her wealth, but one warned Houarn of how many young men had gone there to seek their fortunes and never returned. The traders tried to convince him not to go, but Houarn hired a ferryman to take him to the island.

After traveling across the water, Houarn found himself on a heavily wooded isle. Flowers blossomed, and berries were ripe for the picking. As he walked he found a lake in the middle of the island. At the edge of the lake, he saw what appeared to be a boat shaped like a swan.

The nearer he came to the boat, the more it looked like a swan, until he was close enough to board it. As soon as he did, it came alive. It was a real swan! It ruffled its feathers and kicked its webbed feet, carrying Houarn to the middle of the lake. Suddenly, it plunged into the water and headed for the very bottom.

In an instant, the swan delivered Houarn to the witch's palace, a castle made from crystal and seashells that glittered under the water. Houarn gasped as he marveled at the gorgeous villa. Only then did he realize that he must be under a spell, as he found he could breathe underwater.

Houarn floated up to a towering crystal staircase, which led to the bedroom of the witch.

When he entered, he saw a stunning woman with long auburn hair and skin the color of cream. Her eyes were bluer that the bluest water. Houarn thought that he had never seen anyone so perfect.

The fairy rose and said, "You are welcome here, stranger. I have a place for you in my palace."

Not wanting to be rude, Houarn introduced himself. "My name is Houarn, and I am from Lannilis. I seek my fortune."

The beautiful witch replied, "You may have your heart's desire. I have more than enough to spare." She led the boy into the great hall, where she gave him his fill of wine. But the beverage was enchanted, and soon Houarn fell under her spell.

"How much money do you seek, Houarn?" the witch asked.

"I would be happy with half of your fortune," he answered, forgetting all about Bella thanks to the witch's enchantment.

"You shall have it," exclaimed the witch, "but you must marry me to get it." The spellbound Houarn agreed.

The beautiful witch used her magic to transform the great hall into a banquet wedding feast. For the meal she served fish from a pond by her castle. She brought them into the scullery and began cooking them in a pan. Houarn watched intently, and he started to hear whispers, then murmurs, and finally shouts. They seemed to come from the direction of the pan.

"Who speaks in your pan?" Houarn asked, but the witch only waved him away.

As the spell began to wear off, Houarn wondered why he was marrying the witch when he had a bride-to-be at home. Had he been under an evil spell?

He had little time to think about such things as the witch brought him a scrumptious supper of meats and cheese and a heavenly mushroom soup. Houarn pulled out the knife that Bella gave him and tried to cut up the fish. But the moment his blade touched it, the fish sprang up and became human. He tapped a few more with his knife, and they, too, turned into humans who shouted, "Save us, Houarn. The witch trapped us here and turned us into fish!"

Not knowing what to do, Houarn bolted for the door, but the witch tossed a net over Houarn, trapping him. She then slyly cast another spell turning Houarn into a frog.

Even as this happened, the bell around his neck rang out, clear and loud, and it could be heard many, many miles away. Far away, Bella heard its tinkling. "Houarn is in danger!" She took out her staff and recited the following words:

> "Oh, staff of applewood so fair,
> Lead me on land as well as air,
> Above steep cliffs and over the sea,
> For with my fiancé I must be."

As soon as Bella finished, the staff transformed into a mighty bird whose soft feathers ruffled and unfolded as Bella climbed onto its back. They flew over mountains, forests, beaches, and sea. The giant bird eventually came to rest on a cliff overlooking Loch Isle.

When they landed, a crooked little man no bigger than a bird emerged from a nest and said, "Here is the fair maiden who has come to save me."

"To save you? Who are you?"

The little man replied, "You may not know me, but I can help you. I was once the King of Loch Island, and my wife banished me here."

"Loch Island! That's where I am going. My fiancé is there, and I fear he is in trouble."

The crooked little man replied, "You can help break the spell placed on me, and I will aid you in freeing your fiancé. Go to the palace dressed as a boy and pretend to be in love with the witch. Wait until you find her net and then trap her with it, for it is the only magical thing powerful enough to contain her wickedness."

"That's all fine and well," said Bella, "but I have no boy's clothes." Just when the words left her lips, the little man uttered strange words, conjuring a brilliant white shirt and black trousers.

"Go now, or your gentleman will be hers forever!" said the little man. In a flash, he disappeared, leaving Bella no time to even ask any questions.

Bella mounted her bird, and soon they landed on Loch Island. She, too, found the swan, which took her way down deep under the waters to the witch's castle.

From her balcony, the witch watched Bella dressed as a lad approach the castle. The witch thought to herself, *This strapping young lad is so handsome and possesses such refined clothes. I want him for my husband.*

The witch ran down the stairs and greeted her guest in the same manner that she had greeted Houarn.

Responding just as Houarn had, Bella agreed to marry the witch. Just then, she spied the net. Bella asked, "May I use your net to catch some fish for our supper?" The witch consented, and Bella swiftly threw the net over the witch, who shrieked and seethed in anger, "When I break free, I will hunt you down." However, it was impossible for her to free herself no matter how hard she tried, so strong was her enchanted net.

Looking down, Bella noticed a little frog in the pond beside her, wearing a familiar silver bell, beside an equally familiar knife. Now, she knew that the frog was her love. "My dear Houarn. What has this evil witch done to thee?" Her knife could break most enchantments, and so she touched him with it. Instantly, Houarn transformed back into his human form.

"We must save the others, Bella! The witch has trapped many people here in the form of fish." Bella and Houarn went over to the pond and used the knife to change the fish back into men.

Together, they scoured the castle and came across a vast hall filled to the brim with gems and gold. All they were able to carry with them was one small chest, but it was worth more than enough to make them content for the rest of their lives.

BEHIND THE HOGNEYS, HOUNDS, AND WITCHES— QUESTIONS TO THINK ABOUT

- Was it wrong for Houarn to forget about Bella?
- Did Houarn have a choice in his fate, or was it all the fault of the witch?
- Are heroines as common as heroes? If so, shouldn't they be represented more in myths?

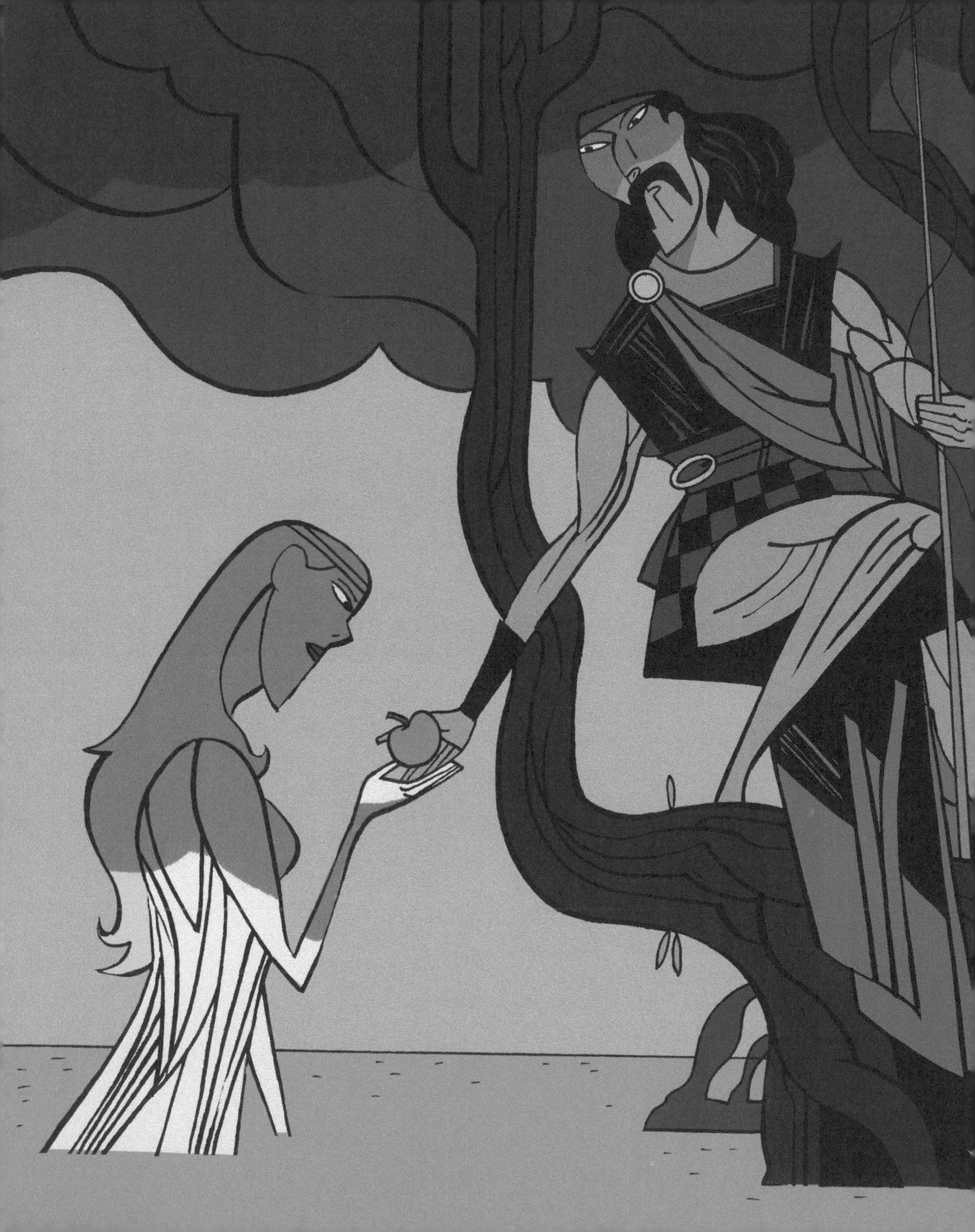

THE TOUCH OF DIRT

(A TOUCH OF CLAY)

—————— *Wales* ——————

In the early days of this world, there were many types of fairies, and some lived in the forests or under the root-covered ground, while others lived under lakes. This is the story of a nymph who lived under Red Lake in the heart of Wales.

A handsome young farmer made his home next to this loch and often would go out on the water to catch fish. One misty autumn day, he could barely see anything, the fog was so thick. But he noticed an old man thatching his roof—under the water. The weather became blustery, the sky clouding and the waters growing choppy, and the farmer was unable to see anything more of the underwater fairy.

Later that autumn, the farmer let his horse drink from the lake. No sooner had his steed's nose touched the clear lake than the farmer glimpsed a young woman, more beautiful than any he had ever seen, on the surface of the water.

Stumbling off his horse, the farmer made his way toward the beautiful vision. But once he got close, the maiden vanished. Even though he looked in every direction, he could not find the entrancing young woman.

Just as he began to believe he had been daydreaming, he saw the young maiden once again. A crown rested atop her hair, and her face was more radiant than any he had ever seen. Her features danced in the ripples of the lake. The beautiful young woman disappeared again and reappeared elsewhere on the surface of the lake five more times, and the young man saw that this was no mere mortal but a fairy. He suspected that the fairy was only playing with him. He went home sadder than he had ever been because he loved her so. He hardly slept, so sharply did he miss her.

Early the next morning, the young farmer hurried to the lake once more, in such a rush that he skipped breakfast and brought a satchel of apples instead. His neighbor had given him the fruit, and the apples were lush and delicious—among the sweetest in the county.

The apples' aroma spread through the air quickly as he crunched and smacked his lips, waiting for her. No sooner had the scent wafted over the lake than the young fairy arose from the waters. This time, however, she seemed much friendlier and requested one of the apples.

"I don't want to throw it to you. It is delicate and might bruise. Come here and get one yourself." The farmer held one of the apples in the air and turned it around so that she could see it, taking in its beautiful blush color and how it looked so juicy. No longer afraid, the fairy glided toward the farmer and gently plucked the apple from his hand. He quickly leapt forward and hugged the woman as she cried out.

No sooner had she screamed than a little old man emerged from beneath the lake, the very man he had seen some months earlier thatching his roof. He had a long white beard and wore a crown of golden lilies. He had to be a fairy, too; otherwise how could he live under the lake?

"Unhand her, mortal!" commanded the old man. "That is my daughter you hold. What do you intend to do?"

"I am sorry, sir and madam. Please forgive me. I don't know what came over me. I was just so entranced by your beauty that I forgot my manners." The young farmer's head hung in shame. "I don't know how this happened, but I feel that I already love you, fair maiden. Would you consider marrying me?"

The old fairy king was a good judge of character. Although the young man had acted poorly in hugging his daughter without her approval, he felt that this was an honest man. He thought long and hard about the proposition. Could he approve of such a union?

"Daughter, this is your decision. I feel that there is no malice in this man, but I cannot make the decision for you. What do you want?"

The young maiden wore a thoughtful look upon her face and was silent for a few moments before she told him, "I will marry you if you swear to always be kind to me." The farmer agreed.

The king made one condition to the union: The young man was never to strike his daughter in any way, not even by accident. Any blow to the maiden would result in her leaving him, regardless of cause or circumstance.

The young man was deeply in love with his future wife. He promised never to hurt her and would do anything in his power to make her happy. The two had a beautiful wedding and were quite a happy young couple. As time went on, the young husband became a sailor, doing work that would help provide a good life.

When he was home, the young husband spent his days caring for his wife. He always did what she asked and gave her little gifts to show her how much he loved her. Soon, the couple had children, and the husband and wife raised them well. The young father taught the children to care for their mother as well as she had cared for them. They were a growing, happy family.

One day, the wife asked her husband to plant a small orchard of the apples that he had given her so many years ago. She longed to taste those sweet apples once again. Surely this was an easy task, and her husband was more than willing to do it. He purchased a tray of apples from his neighbor and quickly sought to plant their seeds, which delighted her more than any other gift he had ever given.

One warm day, they were tending the seedlings, and the wife held the tree while her husband dug a hole in the ground. Several saplings were planted in neat and tidy rows, and all was fine and well. One day, they would bear juicy and sweet apples. But farmers are a superstitious bunch, with a heavy faith in luck. Some plant by the cycle of the moon, while others plant by the position of the stars.

The young woman's husband abided by these customs and in that instant, while he was attentive to her needs, he unconsciously performed an old superstition that led to his ruin.

It had become a habit for farmers to throw the last shovelful of dirt over their left shoulder after they finish planting the last sapling. Such a custom had long been practiced, and farmers didn't even think twice about it.

As the farmer planted the last of the saplings, he mindlessly threw the last clump of dirt over his shoulder, and it hit his wife in the chest. The soft thump sent soil down the front of her dress.

The moment it hit her, the farmer's wife cried terribly, not from pain but from sorrow as she knew that she had to leave her husband. Quick as the wind, she ran to the lake and called out, "Goodbye, dear husband." She leapt into the water, never to be heard from again. Her husband forevermore watches the lake, hoping for his wife's return, which will never come.

BEHIND THE HOGNEYS, HOUNDS, AND WITCHES— QUESTIONS TO THINK ABOUT

- Was it right for the man to hug the woman without her permission?
- Is it fair that the farmer's wife left him because the dirt hit her?
- Can all manner of good works undo a single careless act?
- Was it wise for the fairy king to agree to the marriage after seeing how the farmer had first treated his daughter?

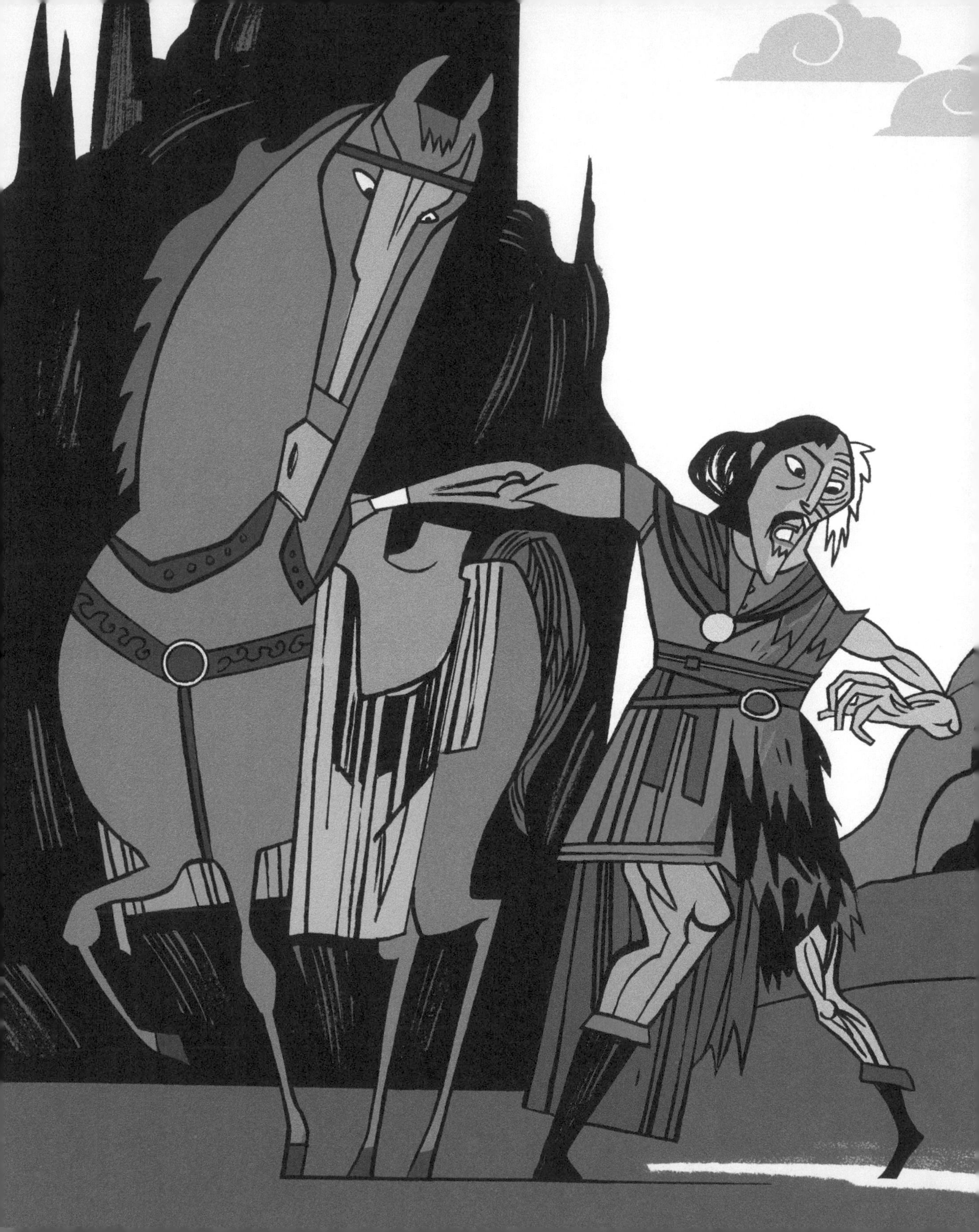

OISIN AND NIAMH

Ireland

In the days when heroes walked the earth, there was a man named Finn. He was but a human, yet he was legendary for his heroic deeds. So it was that Finn came to have a son by a fairy woman, and they named him Oisin. This is the story about how Oisin had a fairy woman propose marriage to him.

One morning on the misty moors of Ireland, Finn and his band of companions known as the *fianna* gathered, saddened by the loss of friends in a recent battle. To lift their spirits, they decided to go hunting in the area around Loch Lein. It was an early spring morning, the flowers were in bloom, birds were chirping, and deer were frolicking in the fields.

Before long, they noticed a stunning young maiden riding through the forest and coming their way. Riding astride an immense white horse, she wore a glimmering crown upon her head and a forest-green silken cloak about her shoulders. Her eyes were a radiant blue that seemed to reflect the distant ocean waves. Her hair was golden—the color of wheat when it is ready for harvest—and her skin was as fair as that of any who had ever walked the earth.

As the maiden approached, Finn could see that she held a bridle attached to the horse with a gleaming golden bit and that her saddle was tooled with gold. The horse wore a crown of the finest silver upon its head.

Surely, Finn thought, *this is not the handiwork of mortal hands.*

The maiden made her way over to Finn and said, "I have had a long journey here, King of the Fianna."

"Who are you, maiden?" Finn asked. "How is it that I do not know your name but you know mine?"

"I am Niamh the Golden-Haired, and I come from a land across the waves. I am the daughter of the King of the Land of the Young."

A hushed silence fell upon Finn and his comrades as they realized she was a fairy maiden.

"Are you fleeing from trouble? Why have you not come with your husband?" asked Finn.

"I am not married," the young princess replied. "Yet I have seen your son, Oisin, from afar and am very fond of him. If he were to have me, I would be his wife."

From the back of the group, Oisin heard the young maiden and was struck by her beauty and spirit. He, too, was in love with her and replied, "I choose you above all women in this world, my queen. I loved you the moment I saw you."

"Then come with me, Oisin. Come to my home in the Land of the Young. You will love being where people don't know the pains of age, where honey flows like water and it is always summer."

Oisin agreed to travel with the young maiden and marry her in her country, but he promised his father that he would return to visit him one day. He bid his companions farewell, mounted the horse with Niamh, and traveled to her homeland.

Finn was sad to see his son leave and bid him farewell. "I will miss you, my son, and fear that I will never see you again."

Niamh and Oisin rode westward all day and night. It was truly an enchanted horse that they rode upon, for it could gallop on the water without sinking. On their journey they saw magical white hounds chasing a hornless white deer and glimpsed cities and houses, islands and dunes, endless mountains, and lush mystical forests.

Eventually, only ocean extended before them. Oisin gazed up at the sky and marveled at the glimmering stars and luminous white moon. Night gave way to day, and the sun grew brighter. Oisin saw grand palaces and vineyards, with every kind of tree and bush. It was a country full of spectacular sights unlike any he had ever seen.

"Is this the Land of the Young?" Oisin asked his soon-to-be bride.

"Yes, my love. You will see that the nation is all that I have described it to be and more."

Upon the couple's arrival, they were greeted at the palace by hundreds of young maidens, and an army of thousands, all draped in gold ceremonial armor, came forth leading the king. Trailing just behind him were the queen and her attendants, all equally young and glowing with health.

"Oisin, son of Finn, you are most welcome here in my land," the king said. "As my daughter's husband, you shall live among us and never grow old as long as you remain here."

That very day, Oisin and Niamh were married in the most extravagant wedding the land had ever seen, and the feast afterward was just as grand. Oisin and Niamh were quite happy with each other.

Over the years, Oisin and Niamh grew closer and closer. They had three children: two sons named Finn and Osgar and a brilliant daughter named Flower.

Time passed quickly in the Land of the Young, and Oisin didn't feel it slipping away as we do in the mortal world. In time, Oisin remembered the promise that he had made to his father. He wanted to see him again as well as his comrades. One evening, he talked with his wife about taking the long journey back to his homeland.

Niamh replied, "You may go, dear husband, but I fear that you will never return."

Oisin assured his wife that he would return, as his steed was the best in the land. He would safely ride to his father's estate and then return home quickly.

"I understand, Oisin," she said, "but the laws of time work differently in our land. If you touch the ground in Ireland, you will instantly become an old man and wither away. So if you go, you can never step off the horse or the years will catch up with you all at once."

"I will heed your words, Niamh. Do not fret. I will be safe."

Oisin mounted the steed and rode to Ireland. His journey was long and tiresome, but no ill befell him. Soon he found himself once again on familiar shores, but so much had changed. The peaceful forests had shrunk and the towns grown so large. Soon a group of townsfolk came out and looked at Oisin with awe. Oisin noticed that they were so small, for so much time had passed that humans had grown shorter while he had retained his size.

Oisin asked if they knew the whereabouts of Finn. While they had heard legends of Finn, he had long since perished. It was only then that Oisin understood that a hundred years had passed while he lived in the Land of the Young. Oisin was saddened to learn that he would never see his father or friends again. Now, they were just memories.

At that moment, Oisin saw a water trough. He wanted to feel his hands rush through the water, longing to feel something from his homeland once again. In his sadness, he forgot his wife's warning and set one foot and then the other foot on the ground. Instantly, his hands withered, and his dark hair thinned and faded to gray. His skin dried and became leathery, and his trusty horse galloped off back home.

Oisin was distraught. His friends had long since perished, and now he had no way of returning to his wife and children. He was lost in the world, not knowing what to do, and so spent the rest of his days as an old man wandering the countryside, reflecting on the memories of his youth.

BEHIND THE HOGNEYS, HOUNDS, AND WITCHES—QUESTIONS TO THINK ABOUT

- Was it unusual for a princess to propose marriage to Oisin, someone she had only seen from afar? Why or why not?
- Like Oisin, should we always strive to honor our word?
- Should Oisin have paid closer attention to his wife's warning?

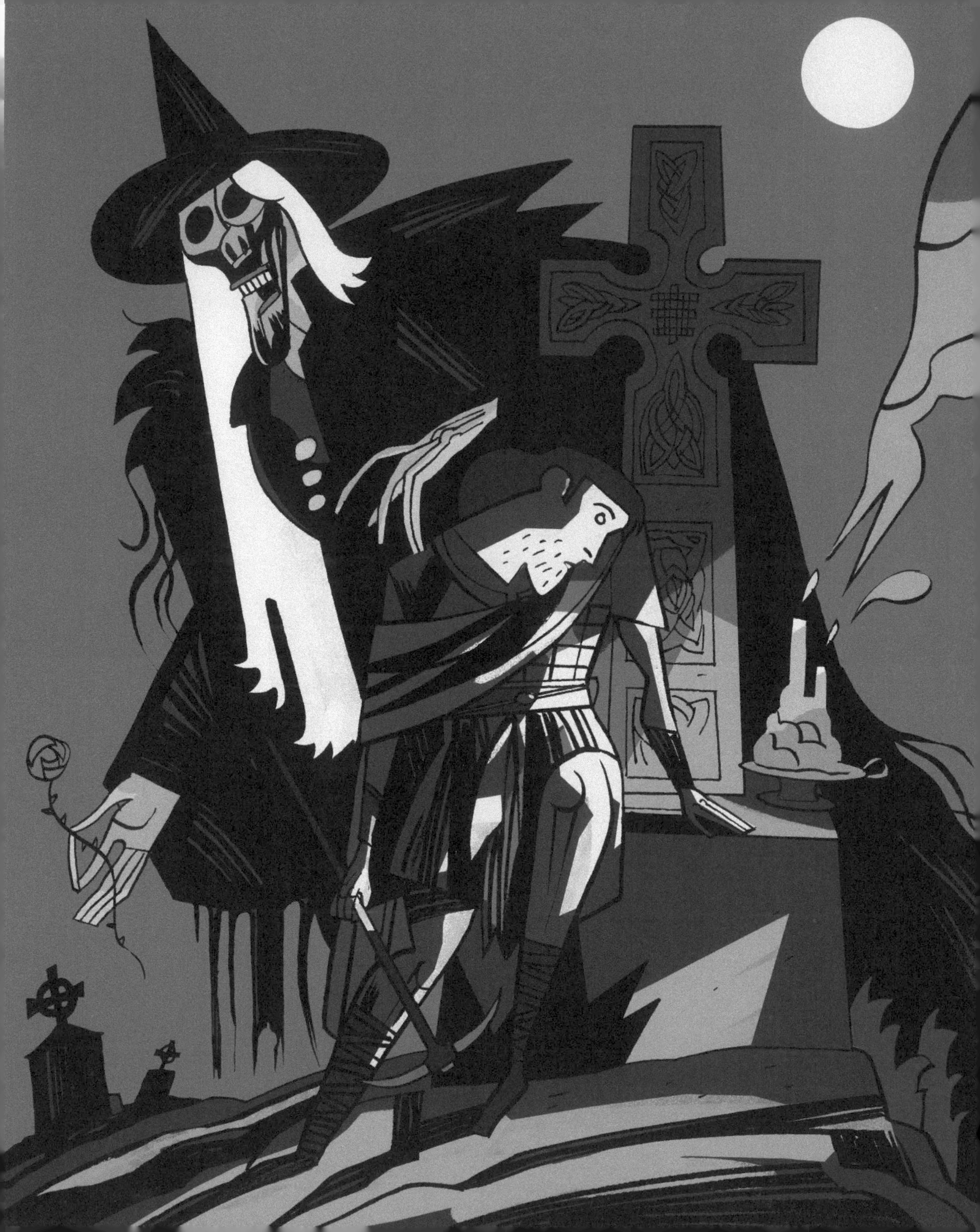

LA ROSE

— *Brittany* —

There was once an older Breton couple who had two sons. The older child went to Paris to seek his fortune while the younger stayed at home. His name was La Rose, and his mother wished him to marry. Finally, he found a bride, but it was to be a short-lived marriage, for she soon took ill and passed away. The young son was devastated. He went to the cemetery every night and wept.

But one night, a dark and dreary phantom approached and asked why he was there.

La Rose, frightened, said, "I am going to pray at my wife's tomb."

"Do you wish she were alive again?" the spirit asked.

"Oh, that is what I desire most!"

"Then let it be so. Return tomorrow at the same hour, and it shall happen," said the spirit. "Just be sure to bring a pick."

La Rose returned the next night with a pick for digging. The phantom pointed to the wife's resting place and, passing him a flower, said, "Break open your wife's tomb and take this rose to pass under her nose. As sure as your name is La Rose, she will wake from her slumber."

La Rose did as the ghost commanded, and, lo and behold, his wife awoke from her slumber, stirring and murmuring, "I feel like I have been asleep forever." The joyous pair embraced and kissed, so happy were they to see each other again. They returned to their home and continued life as if nothing had happened.

But soon, La Rose's father and mother passed away. La Rose wrote to his brother to come home to Brittany to help handle the will. But his brother could not leave, so La Rose left for Paris. He promised to write to his wife, but upon arriving in Paris, he found his brother gravely ill and forgot his promise.

Weeks passed, and without a letter from her husband, La Rose's wife worried that some tragedy had befallen him. Every day, she waited by the mailbox and wept when no letter came.

One day, a group of soldiers came through the town. The captain noticed a beautiful woman across the road who was crying. He asked about her and learned her story. He pined for the beautiful woman, but, alas, she was married. No matter how many flowers he gave her, she paid him no attention.

The captain knew that her husband was in the capital, and as he was fond of the beautiful woman, he wrote a fake letter from

La Rose's brother claiming that her husband had died. The captain paid the woman a visit to console her. So full of grief, the beautiful woman fell in love with the captain, and the two were soon happily married.

Far away, La Rose's brother recovered from his sickness. His cheeks once again grew pink, and his strength returned. And so La Rose returned home, taking the long journey yet pleased to know that his wife would be happy to see him.

It was late at night when he arrived home, and he struggled to open the door. Try as hard as he might, it would not budge. The house was locked, and no one came to the door to open it. La Rose couldn't find any sign of his wife. The neighbors woke and told La Rose that his wife had thought him dead and remarried. How could this have happened? He cried for a long while.

Days passed and then weeks. La Rose had to do something, so he decided to enlist in the army, and as fate would have it, he joined the captain's regiment.

One afternoon, La Rose was writing to his brother when an officer walked by and noticed his beautiful handwriting. The officer immediately made La Rose his secretary.

A few weeks later, the captain visited and spied the secretary's elegant writing. As a favor, La Rose agreed to help the captain with his letters, now and then glimpsing his wife from a distance. But with La Rose in uniform and nearly out of sight, she did not notice him.

One night, La Rose was invited to join the captain for dinner at his home. He stared at his former wife, so caught up in her beauty that he didn't notice a servant slipping a silver platter in his bag. The servant had been planning to steal the platter herself but knew she would be caught. When the platter was discovered missing, the captain searched the house high and low and soon found the platter in La Rose's bag. La Rose was found guilty before the court and condemned to be shot.

While in prison, La Rose became friends with a guard. One day La Rose asked the guard, "Will you do something for me after I die?" The guard agreed as La Rose pulled the magic rose from his jacket. "After I die, go to the cemetery and place this magic rose beneath my nose to awaken me." For this, La Rose paid the man 2,000 francs.

The guard agreed, but when the deed was to be done, he muttered to himself that it wasn't wise to bring La Rose back into this world. He felt that La Rose was at peace. The guard spent nearly all of the money out with his friends, but he began to feel guilty about not honoring his word. He took a pick and headed to the graveyard.

He struck the grave, and it opened to reveal La Rose. The guard was terrified but waved the rose underneath La Rose's nose. As soon as he did, La Rose awoke and muttered, "Good gracious, I have had a marvelous sleep." The guard was astonished and nearly fainted. He could hardly believe that the rose had the power to awaken La Rose from death.

La Rose, free from work, traveled the land aimlessly. One day, he came across a man who worked for the king. The man promised a large reward to anyone who could help the princess, who had years ago been turned into a beast by an evil witch. La Rose felt called to serve the king and help the princess. He would be responsible for guarding the palace at night, even though he learned that every night, the man who guarded the palace would disappear, never to be seen again.

La Rose felt weary as night approached. He was about to flee when a voice called to him and said, "Do not fear, La Rose. I will help you. Soon the beast will appear, but if you lay down your rifle by the sentry box and climb on top of it, no evil will harm you."

Sure enough, La Rose heard the beast at midnight, but he laid down his gun and climbed on top of the sentry box. Although the creature tore apart the rifle, La Rose was not injured. The beast returned to the castle shortly before dawn.

The next morning, the king was happy to see that La Rose was still alive. The king told La Rose that for the spell to be broken, he had to survive three nights.

The next night, the voice gave La Rose different wisdom. "Place your rifle by the chapel door." Again the beast tore apart the rifle but did not harm La Rose. On the third night, the voice told La Rose to open the chapel door and let the beast exit the palace. Then La Rose was to run inside the chapel and hide behind the massive stone altar covered by a red velvet cloth. At the altar he would find a crystal bottle filled with holy water that he could sprinkle on the beast.

La Rose did as he was told and ran inside, barely escaping the beast. He jumped into the shadows and tiptoed behind the altar. The beast smelled La Rose and approached the altar where he was hiding, but La Rose jumped up and sprinkled holy water all over the beast, which instantly transformed back into the enchanting princess. The princess was so happy to have regained her human form and that La Rose had saved her that she fell in love with him and decided to marry him.

As the old ways go, La Rose and the princess were married and lived happily ever after.

BEHIND THE HOGNEYS, HOUNDS, AND WITCHES— QUESTIONS TO THINK ABOUT

- Have you ever felt sadness from not communicating with family or friends?
- Should La Rose's wife have waited longer to confirm his death? How can we know something is true if we have not seen it ourselves?
- Like the guard kept his promise to wake La Rose, should we, too, stick to our word even when we are afraid?

PART

3

LANDSCAPES
in
CELTIC FOLKLORE

To the ancient Celts, the landscape was, indeed, alive.
Within the trees, stones, lochs, and rivers, one could
see fairies, hobgoblins, and leprechauns. These spirits of the land made each and every location unique
and special. This is no different for where you may
live. Different types of sprites and pixies may only be
found in your area. Look with the eyes of your soul,
and you may see them, much as the Celts did.

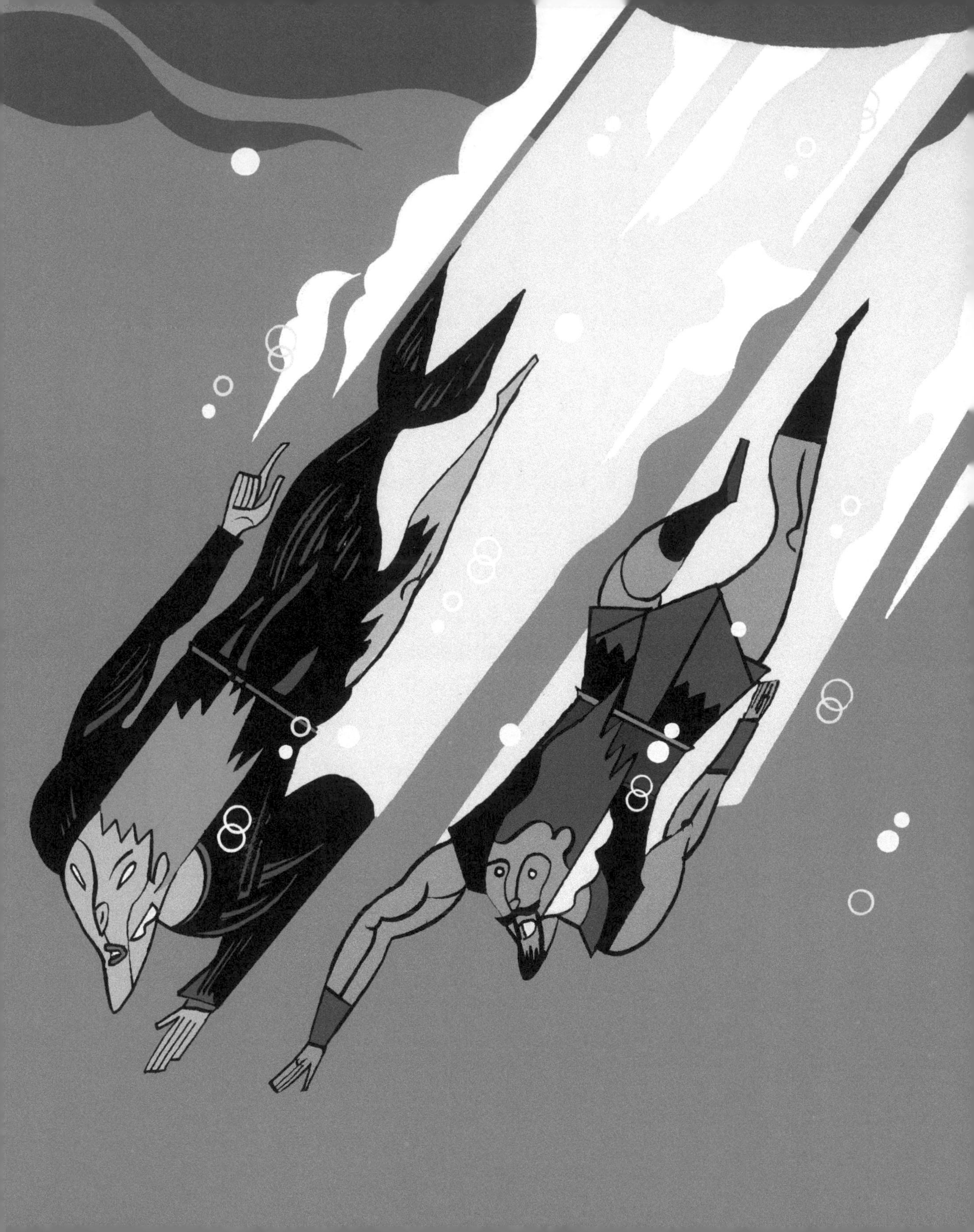

THE
SEAL CATCHER
AND THE
SELKIE

Scotland

Once upon a time in the far north of Scotland, there lived a seal catcher who sold the seals' fur, which in those days was very valuable. This man lived in a small rustic cottage on the seashore.

Seals were more plentiful then and basked in the sun on the beach right by the man's house. However, not all seals were the same, for every so often a colossal seal would come upon the shore to sun itself luxuriously. The common folk would often walk up to the seal catcher and say, "Beware of the *roane*. That fairy looks like a large seal when it is shape-shifting." The seal catcher thought this a superstition and replied, "That is foolish! These seals have massive skins and are the most valuable."

One day when the seal catcher was out working, he wounded a seal with his hunting knife, driving the blade deep enough to stick, yet the seal was very much alive. The creature wailed in pain. Immediately, it dashed back into the sea, taking the blade with it.

The man was very dismayed by the loss of a prized catch as well as the loss of his favorite hunting knife, so it was with sadness that he walked home from the beach. Just as he neared his cottage, a massive man on horseback trotted up to the fisherman.

The stranger asked of him, "Sir, what is your trade?"

To which the seal catcher replied, "I hunt seals for a living."

"Ah, well, it is my lucky day, for I am in need of your services. I need a dozen seal skins if you are able to supply them." The seal catcher was elated, his cheer turning dark once the stranger continued, "I need them this very night."

Without the seal catcher having said a word, the stranger seemed to understand the seal catcher's dismay. "I doubt you have that amount on hand, but I know a place where you can find many seals that are easy to hunt. If you ride with me, I will take you there."

The catcher agreed and climbed onto the horse with the stranger. Together, they galloped to the edge of a tall, steep cliff. "You may dismount, good sir," the stranger called back, "as we have reached the seals." The seal catcher quickly did as he was told and warily approached the drop-off to peer over.

"Where are the seals?" he said.

"You will find out now," replied the stranger. Suddenly, the stranger shed his skin, picked up the seal catcher, and jumped into the sea.

The seal catcher soon realized that the water didn't feel cold on his skin. Even more miraculously, he could breathe! That was when he knew that the stranger was not merely a man but a selkie, with the power to shape-shift from human to seal.

The two descended deeper and deeper into the darkness. At last they found themselves at the gate of a magnificent underwater hall. It was a striking green color and was crafted of sand and mother of pearl. Once inside, the two encountered all manner of selkies. The seal catcher turned to his companion, who, to his astonishment, had turned into a seal. When he looked at himself in the mirror, he also found himself to be a silky-smooth brown seal!

Good heavens! the man thought. *Surely, this stranger placed some enchantment upon me.*

The other selkies in the hall seemed sad and worried. They spoke somberly to one another but never to the seal catcher directly. Eventually his companion found his way back, carrying the knife that the man had lost that very morning.

"Do you recognize this blade?" he asked.

Sheepishly, the seal catcher replied, "I do. It's my knife." Then he sank and pleaded, "Please don't harm me. I didn't know that you were real. I am so sorry. Please, please, please don't harm me."

All of the selkies came about him offering sympathy, saying they meant him no harm. One came up to him and said, "We only want you to heal our king—nothing more, nothing less."

To which the seal catcher replied, "I will if I am able."

The stranger commanded the seal catcher to follow. They passed through corridors until they found themselves in the bedroom of the king. Now this, indeed, was a stout selkie resting on a bed made of seaweed. A bleeding wound could plainly be seen in the king's side. It was clear that the great king was in pain.

"He is my father," said the selkie prince, "You harmed him this morning, thinking he was but a normal seal. You now see that we have the gift of speech and culture, that we have built a great palace, but sadly, we cannot heal him. Only the man who harmed him can heal him."

The seal catcher somberly replied, "I have no skill as a healer, but I will do my best." He approached the king's bed and put his flippers to work trying to close the wound. Although he knew little of the healing arts, his flippers worked like magic, barely grazing the king's side before the wound miraculously closed. Not even a scar remained. The king then sprang out of bed, well once again.

The selkies celebrated their king's recovery by rubbing noses and whiskers with one another, a gesture to show their joy.

However, even while all of the selkies celebrated, the seal catcher could not help but think the worst. He imagined that he was to spend his life as a seal as punishment for his misdeeds. So he was happy to hear from the prince, "You may return home to your wife and children. On one condition."

"Yes, anything. What do you require of me?"

"You must never harm a seal again."

The seal catcher was content with this arrangement as he now recognized that seals had souls, and he pledged his troth by holding up a fin. "I swear on my life that I shall never harm another seal." This was witnessed by all of the sealfolk, who rejoiced. The palace had never had a happier day, as this seal catcher was the most prolific in all of Scotland. Since he had given his word never to harm another seal, they no longer had much to worry about.

The seal catcher prepared to return home. He said goodbye to all of his new friends.

They traveled back through the crystal-clear seawater and soon arrived back on land. Once their skin dried, they changed back into human form. As if by magic, the two jumped the height of the cliff and landed next to their horses, who were nibbling at the grass. The two quickly pulled their clothing back on even though it was soaked by the seawater. Over the hills and through the marshes, the horses galloped to bring the prince and the seal catcher back to his cottage. By morning, they were in front of the seal catcher's home.

The seal catcher extended his hand to shake the selkie's but was met with a hug instead. The prince handed a large bag of gold to the seal catcher and said, "Let it be known that the selkies never take away an honest man's work without making repayment. You honored your part of the bargain, and I am honoring mine."

The seal catcher was shocked. Never had he seen so much gold. There was enough money to keep him, his wife, and their children happy for the rest of their days. The family purchased a stately farm out in the country, away from the sea, and the seal catcher began farming. Since that day, he has only spoken kindly about the selkies and their kingdom and never again picked up his knife.

BEHIND THE HOGNEYS, HOUNDS, AND WITCHES— QUESTIONS TO THINK ABOUT

- Should the seal catcher have heeded the superstition of the common folk?
- Was it wrong for the seal catcher to accept the offer without knowing the terms of the agreement?
- Did the prince make things right by offering the seal catcher gold for changing his job?

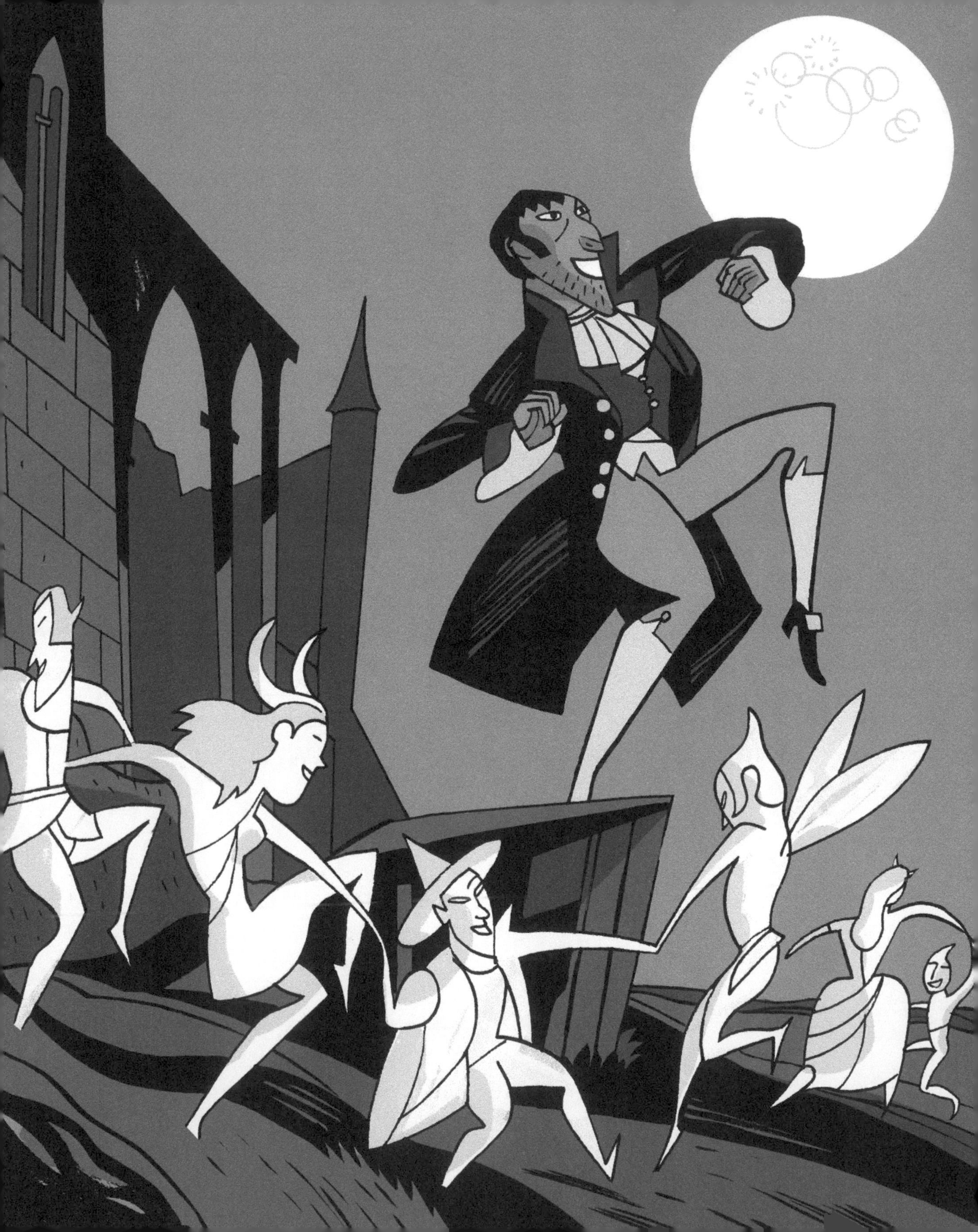

SEVEN YEARS
IN
MERLIN'S CRAIG

——— *Scotland* ———

Nearly 300 years ago, there was a man who lived in the county of Lanarkshire in the lowlands of Scotland. He was a laborer, a jack-of-all-trades worker the Scots called an *orra man*.

One day, this orra man was tasked with going to the moorland to retrieve some peat for the manor. This was not an easy task and meant the man had to pass through an area known as Merlin's Craig, what the Scots called a large rock. Legend had it that the wizard Merlin had once lived in this very place.

The man set about his work, when he noticed a very small, very peculiar woman peeking from around a rock. She wasn't even two feet tall, wore a green dress and red stockings, and had hair the color of flax. The sprite glared menacingly at the orra man, and he abruptly stopped his work. Not knowing what manner of fairy she was or what types of spells she could cast, he was worried.

As if she had heard his thoughts, the fairy sternly said, "You mortals think you can do anything. You stomp about causing all manner of noise. Now you uncover my house. Put that peat back this instant!"

The orra man's mother had taught him all sorts of superstition in his youth, but he hadn't believed they were true. But he did as the fairy demanded and put the peat back exactly where it had come from. He then scurried back to the manor and said, "We should take the peat from the far side of the marsh so we don't bring the wrath of the fairies."

The manor lord laughed, "This fairy is only a figment of your imagination. In order to cure you, go to the marsh now and harvest the peat you returned."

The orra man did as he was told. When he got to the marsh, he was surprised that the fairy was not to be seen and no harm befell him. He began to think that the lord was right and it had all been a dream. Autumn gave way to winter and then to spring and summer. Soon it was autumn once again.

A year to the day from when the orra man had offended the fairy, he was heading back to his cottage and carrying a pail of sweet cream, a reward for all his hard work. He was quite happy with himself and hummed as he walked along. His feet carried him effortlessly down the path so he didn't realize that he was passing Merlin's Craig. Soon he was terribly tired. His eyes began to droop.

I will sit for a few minutes and take a rest, he thought. He sank down on a grassy mound. The moon slowly rose, casting the shadow of the craig upon him. He quickly drifted into a dreamless slumber and did not wake until hours later.

It was midnight, and the moon was high in the sky, lofty and glowing above his head. He rubbed his eyes and opened them to discover that he was surrounded by a band of tiny dancing fairies. They spoke a language of their own that sounded like gibberish to him, but as they twirled about, they cursed him, shaking their fists and mocking the man. He tried to flee but was encircled by the fairies in a magic ring that he couldn't break.

Soon, they tired of insulting the poor fellow. The youngest of the fairy maidens offered her hand to the orra man and invited him to dance. But he was a very poor dancer. Still, some enchantment had been laid upon him, for he could now frolic, leap, and twirl. He was quite amused with himself. The night passed quickly, and the orra man forgot all about his family back home.

At last, a rooster crowed, alerting them that the morning was nearly upon them. The fairies ran toward the craig, and the orra man was caught up among them. He caught sight of a door hewn in the rock where the pixies and fairies were rushing in. He, too, was pushed through the entrance.

Now that he was inside, the orra man saw this was no common passageway—it was an entrance into the fairy kingdom. A massive hall extended before him. Chairs, couches, tables, and ornaments of all kinds filled the passage. Orbs of light lit up the space, and doors ran the length of the hall leading into deeper, darker areas. The man had to sit down to take it all in.

Still under their spell, the orra man made no effort to escape. Instead, he simply watched each sprite go about their work. They cleaned the hall from top to bottom. As the day progressed, they began to prepare dinner. The orra man was quickly approached by a very short elfin maiden clad in green—the same one he had offended the previous year. "The peat you removed from the roof of my house has grown back," she said. "Your punishment was fair, and you have served your term. Now you may leave, but you must not tell a soul what you have seen here." The orra man swore on his honor that he would not tell a living soul about his journey. The door back to the mortal world opened again, and he was given his leave.

While the orra man had been in the fairies' world, he had forgotten about his pail of sweet cream that was standing on the green, though it had long gone sour, smelly, and rancid. He picked it up and hurried home.

When he reached his cottage, he realized that his time in fairyland was far longer than he had guessed, for his wife looked out the door as if he were a ghost. The children whom he had left as mere *bairns* had nearly grown into adulthood. They had no memory of him.

"Where have ye been for so long?" cried the poor man's wife. "I thought ye were dead. How could ye leave us alone like that to fend for ourselves?"

It was only then that he understood that the punishment for removing the peat had been far costlier than he could have imagined.

BEHIND THE HOGNEYS, HOUNDS, AND WITCHES— QUESTIONS TO THINK ABOUT

- Why didn't the orra man heed the warning of the fairy?
- Should the lord of the manor have been more lenient? Why couldn't the peat from the other side of the moor work?
- Was the punishment of the fairies too harsh?

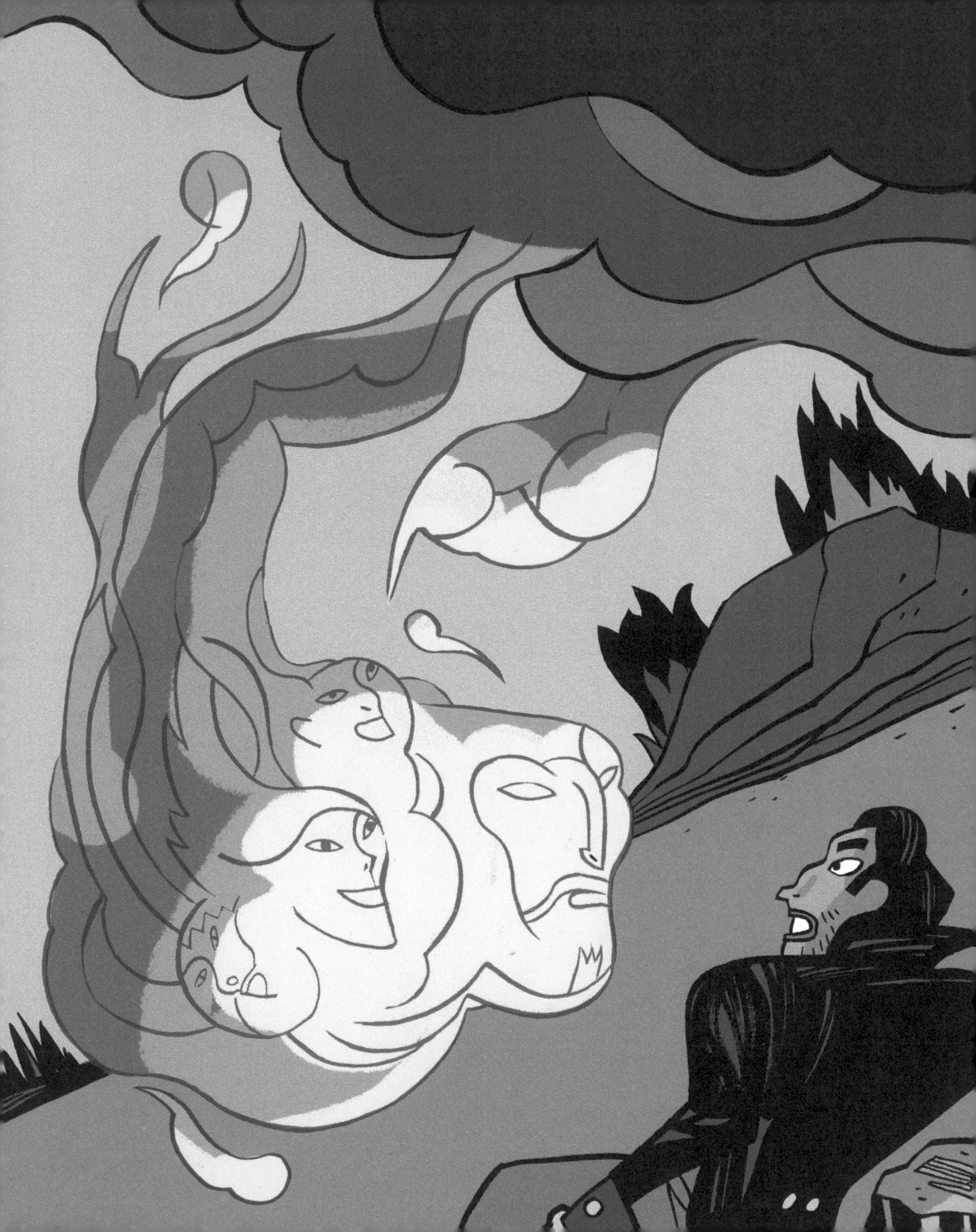

FERGUS O'MARA'S

ENCOUNTER WITH
THE BARROW IMP

Ireland

The Ballyhoura Mountains of County Cork were a place famed in the old days for being home to fairies and goblins. In those times, few humans dared to live in that landscape, for it was the home to fairies and other frightful magical creatures.

Fergus O'Mara was one of the few farmers who dwelled in that country by the southern slope. He lived a simple life and kept to himself. Leading right up to his home was a road that twisted and turned through the hills, and along this path wound a hedge of hazelnut and rowan trees. Their branches crowded out the sun, so the road was frightful to travel both day and night, shadowed and eerie was it at all times of the day.

Not far from Fergus's home sat a wicked goblin's abode. It looked like a small hill with steep rocks and gnarly trees resting upon it. On stormy nights, frightful shrieks and fiendish laughter could be heard from across the mountain. Some years prior, a monk made his way into the mountains, telling Fergus that the hobgoblin of the hollow had its eye on him. Saying very little, the monk only warned that he'd had an encounter with the beast. He urged Fergus to be ever careful to live a blameless life so that the beast couldn't terrorize him. All people in those days knew that if one remained pure, imps could not haunt you, and Fergus never forgot the warning.

But sometimes unfortunate things happen to good people. So it was that one day, one of Fergus's daughters took ill. She was a peaceful youngster and wise beyond her years, but she grew weaker as the days passed. Every day she prayed while holding a blessed candle between her palms. Her parents had no idea what she was doing, but they humored the girl. At last, the young child passed away. It was with such peace that one could barely tell she had passed on, and her parents were very sad.

One year later, it was approaching Halloween. On a warm October morning, Fergus set off to church, an open-air chapel since the townsfolk did not have the gold to build a church. On this day, in particular, Fergus set out alone.

As Fergus walked down the lane not far from the imp's hill, he heard the yelping of hounds, and a roebuck deer pranced across the road with dogs hotly in pursuit. It is likely that throughout all of Ireland, Fergus was the one who loved hunting the most.

As he was on his way to church, he didn't have much time to spare. But the hounds' barking let him know that they were close to catching the deer, so Fergus dashed off to chase the deer, the hounds, and the hunt. Through the fields and dales they went, and before long the entire morning had passed.

Church was over, and the villagers now returned home, talking of Fergus, who had never missed Mass. His wife and children soon came back, finding the cottage empty and the last of his porridge gone cold.

Meanwhile, Fergus was in the fields close to the upland moors. Just on the edge of the wildlands, the hounds and deer passed behind a large rock, and he lost sight of them. Suddenly, the dogs cried. Their yelps gave way to an unholy cackling, which Fergus had heard come from the imp's mound many times before. It was at this moment that Fergus sat on a boulder and thought about his deeds.

Why had he gotten so caught up in the hunt? Why did he forget about his family and Mass? Was this the very day that the monk had foretold so many years ago? Had the imp lured him away? Fergus quickly rose and made his way back home, hoping to get there before dusk.

He was nearing the halfway mark when night fell. The weather began to change, and wind and rain descended from the north, bringing along lightning and thunder. It became hard to see. Fortunately, Fergus was familiar with the terrain and traversed the mountain. But then he came close to the imp's home.

Laughter and shrieks burst forth from the mound, the very same he had heard when he had lost sight of the hounds. An unholy and dark cloud billowed forth from the entrance to the barrow-mound. With an immense gust of wind, it came shrieking and sweeping toward him. He ran toward home, but no matter how hard he tried, the cloud gained on him. Glancing back as he ran, he saw all manner of ghostly faces and heard voices coming from the cloud.

The darkness was almost complete when suddenly a bright light shot across the sky and floated down between Fergus and the cloud. There he saw a little child, *his child*, his precious little daughter who had left this world. She looked as radiant as she ever had, with blonde hair and a brightly lit candle in her tiny hands. The more the storm raged, the more the candle glowed. Fergus's daughter had come to save him.

The imp within the cloud shuddered at the brightness, still tormenting Fergus, who began running once more. His child followed behind, between her father and the imp as if she were acting as a guardian. At this point, the imp was furious, and the wind grew even more intense. A whirlwind twisted upon itself and tore the ground below it. All the while, the child continued to guard her father.

As Fergus approached his home, he could see that his family had left the door halfway open. They had been expecting him, surely. His family looked on, afraid of the approaching din. He rushed forward, falling flat on his face as he leapt through the door. Then with a violent slam, the door was bolted shut by some unseen force. Fergus's wife rushed to her husband and lifted him up. Outside, the tempest tore across the ground, uprooting plants and trees alike and throwing them this way and that.

At last the noises began to quiet. One could hear that the storm had moved on. The night was soon still.

With daylight the next morning came evidence of the wild happenings of the night before. Rocks, trees, and bushes littered the landscape. It looked as if the world had come to an end, but the bright morning sunlight showed that this storm, too, had passed.

From then on, Fergus never failed to meet his obligations. He never ventured back to the mound, even though neighbors said that the imp had removed itself to some other county. Quiet and simple once more, he had a happy life.

BEHIND THE HOGNEYS, HOUNDS, AND WITCHES— QUESTIONS TO THINK ABOUT

- Should Fergus have followed through with his obligations?
- Was Fergus's daughter his guardian angel?
- Does love (or right) always win over evil?

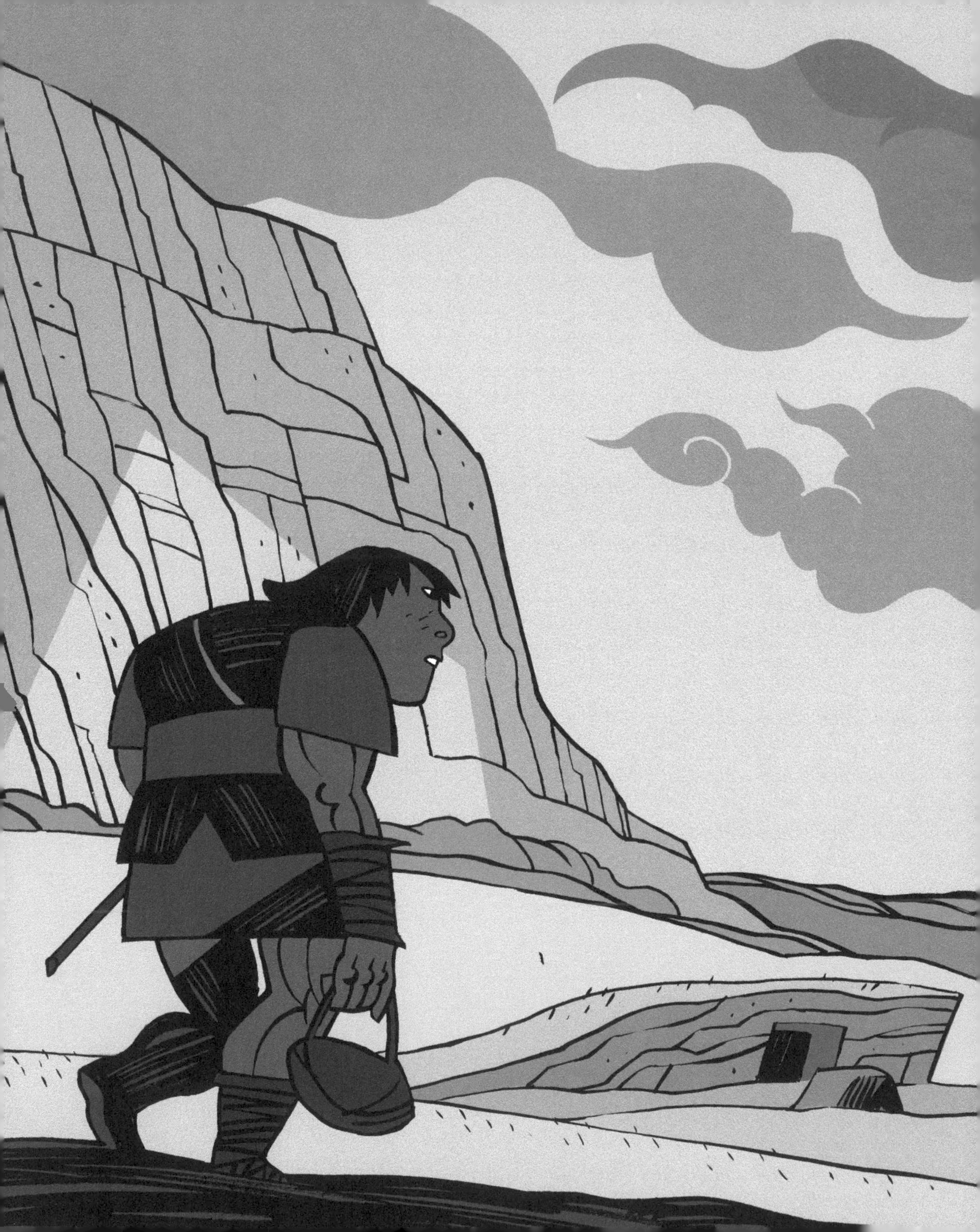

SNORRO OF THE
DWARF STONE AND THE
TWO EARLS

Scotland

Far to the north of Scotland on the Island of Hoy stands a vast boulder. Long ago it was home to a dwarf named Snorro. His father was a fairy who had given his son the gift of eternal youth. His mother was mortal, and from her he inherited ambition and vanity. He was a handsome dwarf, so he often carried an enchanted mirror that he gazed into for long hours.

Snorro passed many of his years studying the art of herbalism. He made medicines from herbs that he collected from all around the island. Because of this, the local inhabitants would come to him for help with their ills. But so vain was he that he required visitors to bow to him as if he were king. And because they needed his remedies, they did so.

The dwarf was well adept at all aspects of divination—the magical process of trying to see the future. He owned a black leather-covered book that was said to contain many secrets. It was even said that Snorro would consult his book and tell the fortunes of those who visited him.

But few could honestly guess why Snorro chose to live in a large boulder so far away. Some said that his home concealed a magical crystal that could bring health, wealth, and happiness to its owner. Snorro spent his time keeping an eye out for this red gemstone. At night he would search for the gem accompanied by his pet raven, an inky black bird the villagers looked upon with suspicion and dread.

During this age, Orkney, a group of islands in the north of Scotland, was ruled by two brothers, both of whom were earls. One was named Paul, the other Harold. They were very different rulers. Paul was mild-mannered, and the people loved him. Harold was jealous and quick to anger. The townspeople disliked Harold, and he knew they liked his brother better, which made him even more insecure.

One day Earl Harold went to Scotland with his mother, Countess Helga, to visit the Scottish king. While there, a young Irish woman caught his eye. Her name was Lady Morna, and she was quite beautiful. One glance at her, and Harold knew he wanted her as his bride. With much excitement, he ran up to her one day, extended his hand with a ring, and asked, "Would you be my bride, Lady Morna?"

This was, indeed, a great honor, but she replied, "I am sorry, Harold, but I am not in love with you."

Harold was furious, but he sought to change her mind through guile. He invited Lady Morna to Orkney to visit. Once she arrived on the island, she was greeted by Harold's brother, Paul.

"Lady Morna, it is a pleasure to meet you," Paul said.

Bashfully, she replied, "The pleasure is mine."

The two instantly felt something spark between them. They often sought each other out to talk and enjoy each other's company in private. But this was not to remain hidden. Once Harold found out about Paul and Lady Morna, he was blinded by jealousy and nearly stabbed his brother. But he was calmed by his brother's words when Paul said, "Surely, I care for the maiden, but why would she choose me when she could have you?"

Harold was flattered and apologized for his temper.

Now it was nearing Yule, and it was custom during that time for the earl to leave Kirkwall and head to the Palace of Orphir for celebrations. Paul readied for his journey. That afternoon, he came across Lady Morna sitting by a large window looking out at the party that was about to leave. He saw sadness in her eyes, and he felt sad, too.

"I wish not to be parted from you," Paul said mournfully.

"You have duties to attend to. But I, too, wish that we could stay with each other forever," Lady Morna replied.

At the same time, the two both said, "I love you!" Happy tears began to flow as they embraced one another.

But knowing how wicked and jealous Harold was, they knew that they must keep their love secret. They decided to wait until after Yule to tell the family, but it was not to be so. Paul's aunt, the wicked Countess Fraukirk, was hiding behind the curtains listening. She had long hated Paul for being unworthy of her family and no relation of hers. Now that he had won the love of Lady Morna, rage filled her. So she ran off to her sister's chamber, where the two talked all night, scheming to put Helga's son, Harold, in Paul's place.

The next morning, Countess Fraukirk wore a heavy cloak and sat in a boat that was speeding over the watery channel. She had often sought out Snorro's help with spells and enchantments, and the wicked dwarf already knew the woman's ill intent. "I am sorry, but I cannot help you, Countess," he said when she reached his boulder. "I will not help you do this evil thing to Paul. If they knew I had done it, I would have to flee." Countess Fraukirk offered more and more money and even a position in the king's court before Snorro agreed to create the spell.

He wove a magical cloth, one that would kill anyone who wore it. The countess was to make a waistcoat from it that she would give to Paul as a Yule gift. Meanwhile, back at the castle, Harold offered his heart once again to Lady Morna, pleading, "Lady Morna, I love you more than anything. Please marry me. I will not be happy until we are wed."

"I am sorry, Harold, but I don't love you. I am in love with another, your brother Paul."

Harold flew into a jealous rage. He quickly mounted a horse and rode toward the sea, seeking a love potion from Snorro. Harold hired a boat and soon made his way to the Island of Hoy and then up the hillside. There he found Snorro at the mouth of his cave, his pet raven perched upon his shoulder. Harold bartered with the dwarf and paid handsomely for the love potion. He sped back to the castle, his potion in hand.

Harold now sought to deposit the potion into Lady Morna's cup. It took two days to find the right chance, but he finally did so. Lady Morna had seen Harold gazing at her cup, so she only pretended to drink. And when Harold wasn't looking, she tossed it away. Harold simply waited for the potion to work its magic. In the meantime, Lady Morna was overly kind to Harold, biding her time until Paul returned.

When Paul returned on Yule Eve, Harold knew that the love potion had not worked, for Lady Morna was still truly in love.

Upstairs, Countess Fraukirk and her sister were about to wrap the deadly gift for their nephew. Harold burst in, glimpsing the beautiful waistcoat of silver and gold, and he was enchanted by it. "For whom have you made that?" he cried.

To which the countess replied, "'Tis a gift for Paul."

Angrily, Harold yelled, "'For Paul?' Why is everything for Paul?" He snatched up the garment and ran out. The countesses tried in vain to warn him. But he had put it on, and the poison had already done its deed. He fell to the ground in great pain as his brother found him.

"I wronged thee, brother," Harold said. "Beware of my mother and her sister. They were trying to kill you." With that Harold passed away.

The two sisters fled to the mainland, hoping to escape Paul's revenge. They were nearly caught by the palace guards, but in the end their wickedness was met with a tragic end, for the Vikings burned down their castle with the sisters inside.

Knowing none but Snorro could be behind such wickedness, Paul made his way to the island and Snorro's boulder. But he found it abandoned. It is said that the spirits of the air had taken the dwarf away, imprisoning him for his evil deeds.

Lady Morna became Countess Morna upon marrying Earl Paul, and they lived the rest of their days in peace and contentment.

BEHIND THE HOGNEYS, HOUNDS, AND WITCHES— QUESTIONS TO THINK ABOUT

- Why was the stepmother so cruel to her stepson?
- Can jealousy blind someone and hurt their relationships with others?
- How might things have been different if the dwarf had used his powers for good?

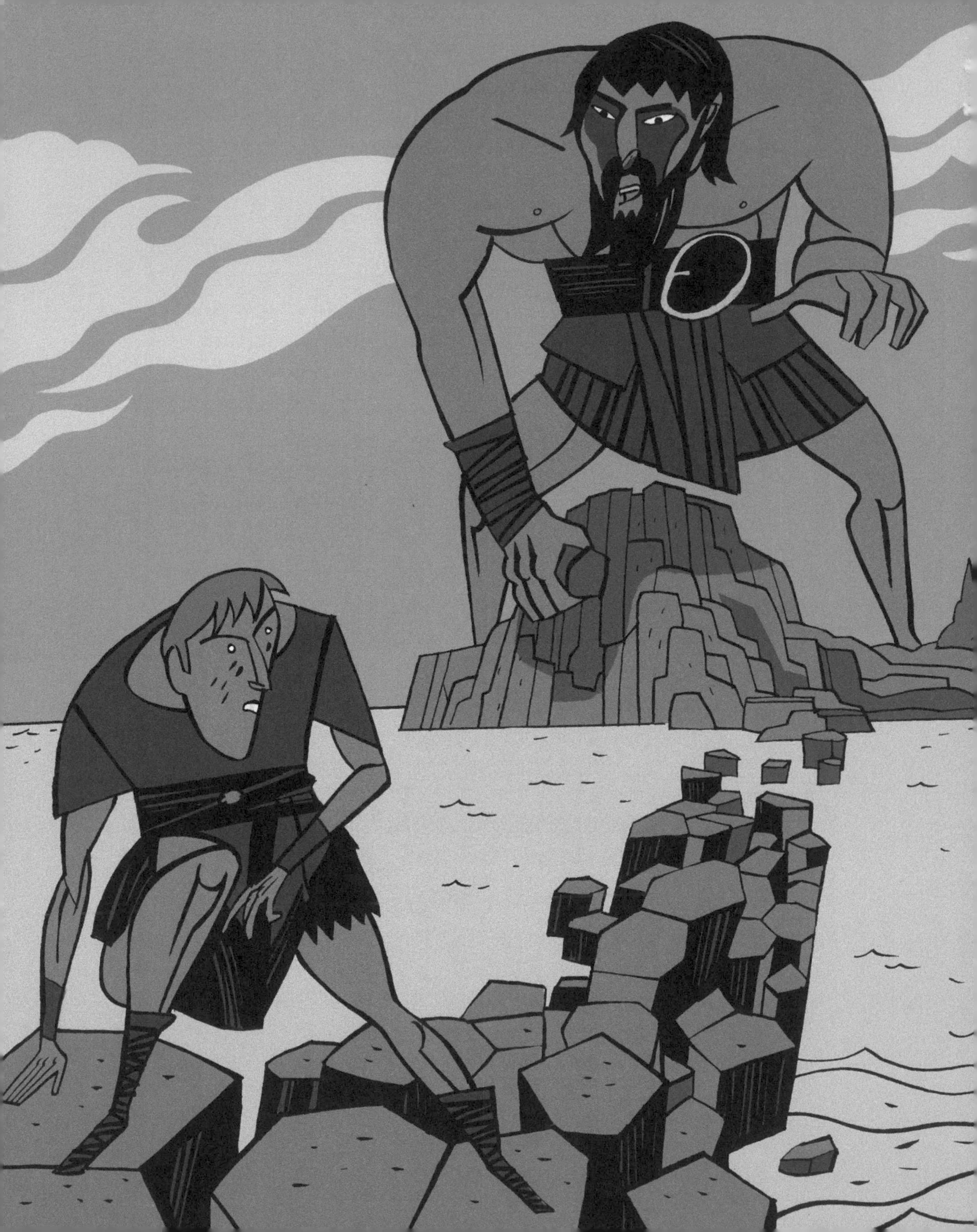

THE GIANT'S CAUSEWAY

Ireland

In the north of Ireland lived the foster mother of the legendary hero Finn Mac Cumhaill. Years before, Finn had eaten a magical salmon and earned the gift of divine inspiration.

One day while Finn was visiting his foster mother, he decided to take a break and look out over the ocean. In the distance he could see Scotland, and much to his astonishment he could see a humongous giant. It seemed that the giant was building something in the water. The enormous figure then looked at Finn and bellowed across the water, "I'm coming for you, Finn. I have heard of your strength, but now you will meet your match."

The giant did look menacing, but Finn was not afraid. "Come over any time. I don't fear you," he said. No more was said between the two. The giant went back to his work, and Finn returned to the cottage.

Finn's friends had always boasted of their leader's abilities, and it appeared that word had reached the giant. Finn felt like he had nothing to fear as he had already bested every man in Ireland.

Over the next few weeks, Finn went to see the progress that the giant was making on building the causeway (bridge) across the channel. As he did so, the giant came closer and closer to Ireland. Finn could now gauge the height of the man, who was at least four times his size. He watched the giant slam stones into the water and became uneasy, his stomach flipping and flopping. Finn wasn't a coward but was smart enough to understand that there was little chance of winning in hand-to-hand combat with this beast of a man. So he drew up a plan.

When the giant had nearly completed the work, Finn kept out of sight and called upon his foster mother's help. She made a large ball of whey from curdled milk and placed it beside a stone. Then she kindly made *bannocks* (oatmeal cakes)—some were soft, and some had iron plates baked inside. Once they were ready, Finn told her his plan for besting the giant. Using his magical gift, he knew that the giant's strength came from one of his fingers, even though he could not discover which one was magic.

On the day the giant finished the bridge, the very same day, Finn dressed as a baby and settled into a large crib, all part of his plan.

Eventually, the shadow of the giant filled the doorway. He bellowed, "Where is Finn Mac Cumhaill?" His voice made the walls of the house tremble. Finn's foster mother remained calm and rocked the baby cradle. She looked over at the giant and asked, "Who are ye?"

"That's no worry of yours," he boomed. "I have come from Scotland and have business with Finn."

"Oh, ye must be that poor fellow who wants to fight with Finn," the woman said.

"'Finn will be the poor one when I get through with him," the giant grumbled.

The woman invited the giant in and apologized for the fact that Finn was not present. "Finn will be back tomorrow," she said. "He waited as long as was possible, but he asked you to stay, for he didn't want to miss ye."

The giant made himself at home while the woman readied some food for him to eat. She stirred the weak fire as the giant got comfortable.

As he peered around the room, the giant saw the cradle. "Who is that?" he asked.

"Oh, that's just Finn's baby boy," the woman replied. "Now if you could just be a bit quieter, the baby is teething. If you wake him, he will surely cry."

After some time, the woman kept stirring the coals, but the fire would not light. She said, "The wind is going in the wrong direction. If Finn were here, he would turn the house around so it would blow in the right direction."

The giant laughed, "I can do anything Finn can." With haste, the giant went outside and turned the house around as if it were a top. He went back inside and asked, "How did I do?"

To which the woman replied, "The fire is much better now, but you did it a bit clumsily. Finn would have done it better." This took the wind out of the giant's sails.

The woman saw she was out of water and asked the giant to rip apart the spring rock, as Finn had promised to do for her. The woman led the giant to where two peaks were close together. The giant placed one foot on one summit and pushed with his hands against the other to shove them apart. The spring welled up, and water gushed. But still the woman showed no sign of wonder at the giant's might. This began to dishearten the giant.

Seeing a large rock that the woman had placed on a shelf, he wondered, "What is that stone for?" The woman replied, "Oh, Finn practices squeezing water from that rock in the mornings. It helps him keep up his strength."

Taking up the stone, the giant tried his own hand at extracting the water, but squeeze as hard as he might, no water came forth. Far below the giant, the woman saw that the little finger on his left hand squeezed tighter than any other.

She said, "If all of your fingers were as strong as the little one, you could extract some water, no doubt."

The giant replied, "Ay, good woman, but that is where my strength is stored."

The baby gave out a cry, and the woman murmured. "He feels sorry for you! Even he can squeeze water from the rock. His father lets him practice already." The old woman passed the stone made of whey to the baby. Finn took it and squeezed, and water poured to the floor. The giant began to feel uneasy. Surely if the baby was that strong, his father must be intensely powerful.

Over the crackling fire, Finn's foster mother finished warming the oat cakes and handed one with iron to the giant. He bit into it and immediately broke a tooth. He grumbled, but the woman just remarked how Finn didn't like the oat cakes because they were too soft. This made the giant want to eat another, so the woman handed him one more. He promptly chomped down and broke more teeth. Spitting them out, he wondered, "Finn doesn't like these because they are too soft?"

"Yes. He leaves them for the baby to eat." She took one of the oat cakes that didn't have an iron core and gave it to Finn, who quickly ate it up. It astonished the giant.

"You say the baby is just getting his teeth?"

Taking an oat cake of her own, the woman nodded. This perplexed the giant, so he went over to the baby to feel such hard teeth. When the little finger containing the giant's power got close to Finn's mouth, Finn chomped down and bit it off. The giant writhed in pain, but Finn quickly got up and chased him out of the house. With his long legs as tall as trees, the giant crossed over the bridge before Finn could get there. The giant then tore apart the bridge, leaving just a small section on the Irish side, which is now called the Giant's Causeway. As you might expect, the giant never came to Ireland ever again.

BEHIND THE HOGNEYS, HOUNDS, AND WITCHES— QUESTIONS TO THINK ABOUT

- Should Finn's friends have boasted about his strength?
- Do brains always win out over brawn? Was Finn's plan a good one?
- Could Finn have talked it over with the giant and avoided the fight altogether?

INTO THE WIDE AND WILD WORLD

The Celtic people lived close to the natural world surrounded by vast wilderness. Because of this, it was common for Celtic myths and folklore to be filled with stories of adventure in the mountains, forests, and sea. What these tales symbolize is how life is an adventure and how in growing up we battle our inner monsters, overcome challenges, and find out who we really are. It is a journey of self-discovery.

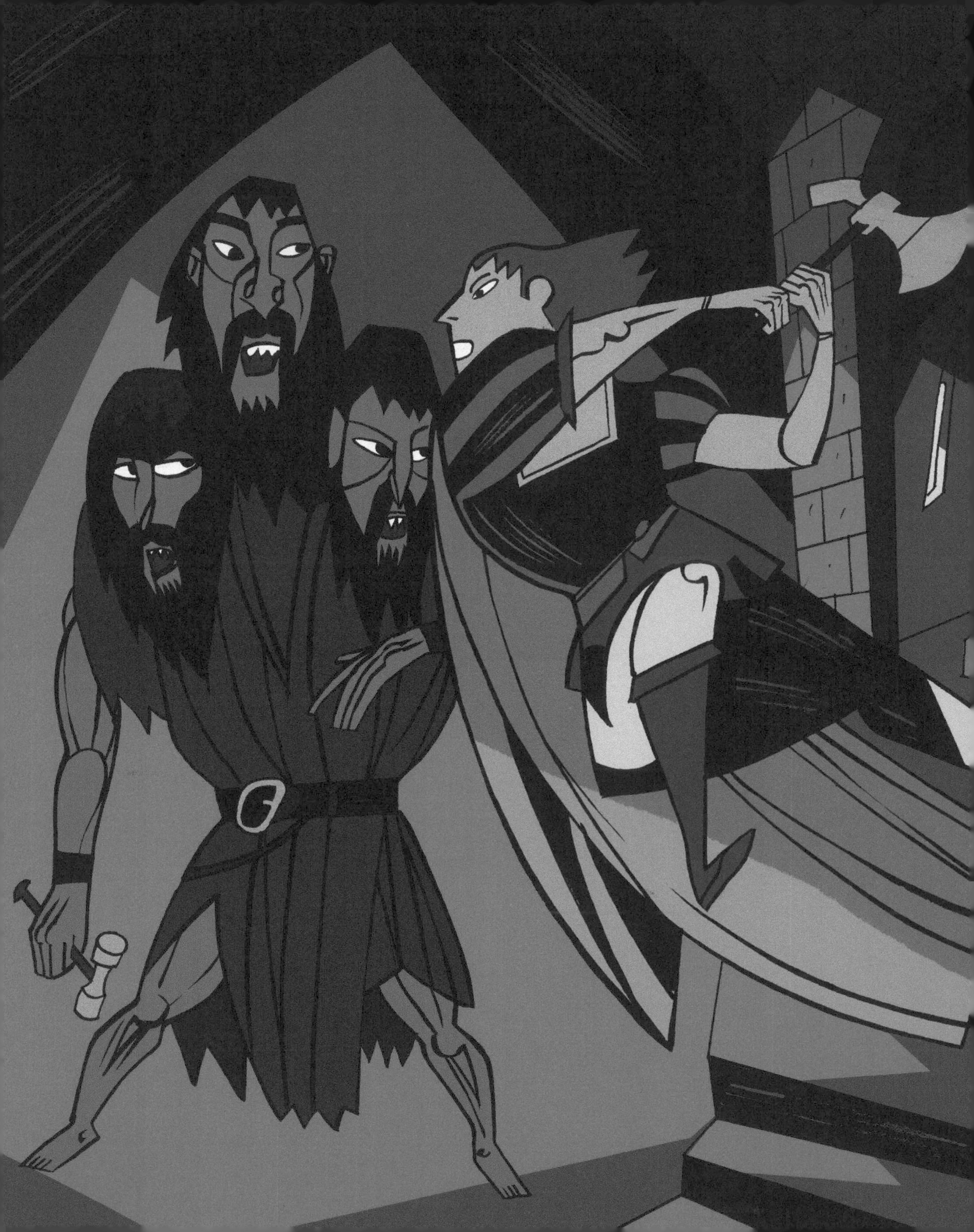

THE
RED ETIN

Scotland

Far in the north of Scotland, near the land of King Malcolm, there lived two widows in cottages next door to each other. Each woman had rolling lands where sheep, cows, and chickens grazed, which is how they and their families survived. The children of the widows were the best of friends and played with each other. There were three in total, for one widow had two boys and the other had one.

Soon the eldest of the three came of age and needed to make his mark on the world. Before he left home, his mother said to him, "I shall make you a cake to send you off into the wide world!" and so she had him fetch water from the well, and she said, "However much water you bring back will decide the size of the cake I bake for you."

The eldest boy ran and ran, but with a leaky bucket, even as he reached home there was very little water left.

The mother told her son, "You must make a decision to take half of the cake and go with my blessing or take the whole cake but without my approval."

Although the son wanted his mother's grace, the cake was small and the journey long, so he said, "I want your blessing, but the cake is so tiny. I will take it all. I hope to return and make you proud."

Before the boy left, he went to his younger brother and gave him his hunting knife, an enchanted one. He said, "If the blade stays pristine, you will know I am safe, but if it rusts, evil will have fallen upon me." Then he set out on his journey.

After a few days, he came across an old man and a flock of sheep. The boy thought to himself, *Perhaps I will tend to these sheep and earn my way.* And so the lad asked the old man, "Who owns these sheep, good sir?"

The man responded, "They belong to the Red Etin of Ireland."

The young lad didn't think that this giant *etin* sounded like a man he wanted to work for, and so he traveled onward. Eventually he came to a man with snow-white hair who attended a herd of swine. Again, the lad asked, "Who owns these pigs, good sir?"

The man replied, "They belong to the Red Etin of Ireland." At this point the boy began to get frustrated and wondered when he would find new lands that were not owned by the Red Etin. He went on his way again.

Soon the lad had run into the oldest man he had ever seen, a twisted old fellow who was herding goats. The lad asked yet again, "Who owns these goats, good sir?"

The old man advised, "These goats belong to the terrible three-headed Red Etin. He is larger than a building." But he added, "Up till now you have only seen animals that cannot harm you; however, if you travel further you will find beasts that are dreadful in nature."

"Thank you for your advice, good sir," said the lad and went on his way.

Before long, the lad ran across a herd of three-headed creatures with gnashing teeth and terrible eyes. He was so frightened that he ran as fast as his legs would carry him, through the hills and dales he ran, up to a magnificent castle. The door stood wide open, and so he ran in. He walked the halls and rooms and found an old woman in the kitchen. She was warming herself by the fire, with her feet stretched toward the glowing coal.

"May I stay here tonight?" he asked of the woman.

"You may stay," the old woman replied in a hushed voice, "but this is the home of the Red Etin, and so we must hide you." She glanced around cautiously, for it was dark outside, and if it had not been pitch-black, the lad would have been in even more terrible danger.

The old woman hid him in a closet under the stairs. It was a quaint but comfortable space nestled into the cozy shadows of the hushed house. The boy was nearly asleep when he heard a bellowing voice upstairs:

"I seek out, and seek then,
I smell the bones of a human!
If he is alive, or if he is dead,
I will make him into bread."

The lad shook in fear. All throughout the castle, it sounded like a beast rifling through cupboards. Eventually, the door to the closet flung open, and there the Red Etin stood. The young lad pleaded for his life, yelling, "Please don't hurt me. I only needed shelter for the night."

Now even Etins operate under rules, and so the Red Etin told the lad that if he could answer three questions, he could walk free.

For the first question, the Etin's first head asked, "Was Ireland or Scotland first inhabited?" The boy didn't know, and so he stayed quiet.

For the second question, the Etin's second head asked, "How old was the world when Adam was made?" Again the lad had no idea how to answer, and so he stayed quiet.

Lastly, the Etin's third head asked, "Were animals or humans created first?" He was clever but not wise, and so the boy could not answer. Pulling an odd little hammer from his pocket, the Etin tapped him once and instantly turned the lad into stone.

Back at home, the younger brother looked at the knife on the third day and saw that the enchanted blade looked rusty, dull, and dimmed. He knew he must journey to find out what had befallen his brother. Like his sibling, his mother charged him with getting water for a cake to send him off. Like before, he came back with very little water and chose the whole cake over his mother's blessing.

On his journey, he ran into the same old men and animals and heard the same warnings of the Red Etin and the terrible beasts. And at last he found the three-headed creatures and ran to the Red Etin's castle. The old woman hid him in the cupboard under the stairs, but the Etin smelled him, too. He asked him the same questions and turned him into the same stone. But this time, just outside the Etin's castle window, a kind fairy waited and watched and heard what happened.

Swiftly the fairy flew and brought the news to the widow who lived next to the missing boys. Her son knew he must find his friends, but he was different than the first two boys. When he fetched water for the cake, he patched up the pail so that the water remained in the bucket. He was a kind and loyal boy, and so he chose to take half of the cake with his mother's blessing instead of the whole cake.

The young man then went on his way. He walked a good long while and then pulled out his cake to eat. Somehow, it seemed a larger cake than he had remembered.

At that moment, a poor old woman walked by and asked of him, "I am hungry, young master. Would you spare an old woman a bite to eat?" The boy was starved, but his disposition was so kind that he gave the old woman half of his cake. In an instant, moved by his kindness, the woman turned into a fairy, and she warned him, "Many dangers lay ahead. Please take this wand." She handed him an enchanted wand and whispered into his ear about how to avoid any harm that might come his way.

Like the boys before him, the young man encountered the same old men and animals. But when he came to the three-headed creatures, he was not afraid. One of the creatures charged at him, but the boy simply struck it with the wand, and it disappeared.

Soon the boy arrived at the castle but still he felt no fear. The old woman hid him as she did the others, but when the Etin found him, the boy was still not afraid. The monstrous Etin dwarfed the boy as he pulled him from the closet. Then he bellowed, "Boy, answer my questions correctly and you will live, but if you can't you will perish like those before you."

Much to the chagrin of the giant, the lad answered the first question correctly. The Etin yelled, "How did you know that?" and grunted in frustration. When the boy answered the second question, the Etin screamed, "Someone must be helping you! No fair!" Then, his voice a mix of anger and fear, the Etin shrieked when the boy answered the third question correctly, too.

The Etin knew then that his power was gone, but he still tried to beat the boy. The lad took out an ax, and the two fought. While the Etin was still large, he no longer had power in him. The boy got the upper hand and swung the ax into one of the Etin's heads. With one swift chop, the giant fell down dead, and with that blow, the enchantment on the castle was broken.

From behind the Etin, a secret door sprang open, and a young maiden came forth, no longer held by the Etin's magic. She was a radiant beauty and King Malcolm's daughter. The two youths instantly fell in love.

Together, they journeyed to the dungeon, where he found two people-shaped stones, the brothers and his best friends, and he tapped them with his wand, instantly changing them back into their human forms. The group departed the castle and traveled to King Malcolm's realm along with the princess.

The king could see how much love his daughter had for her rescuer, and he was so thankful for her return that he made the boy a prince. A marriage commenced the next day, and the whole kingdom celebrated. They were to live happily ever after.

BEHIND THE HOGNEYS, HOUNDS, AND WITCHES— QUESTIONS TO THINK ABOUT

- Can being kind change the course of our fate?
- How can friends watch out for each other and assist each other in times of trouble?
- Can two people approach a situation differently and receive different results, such as the way the boys did?

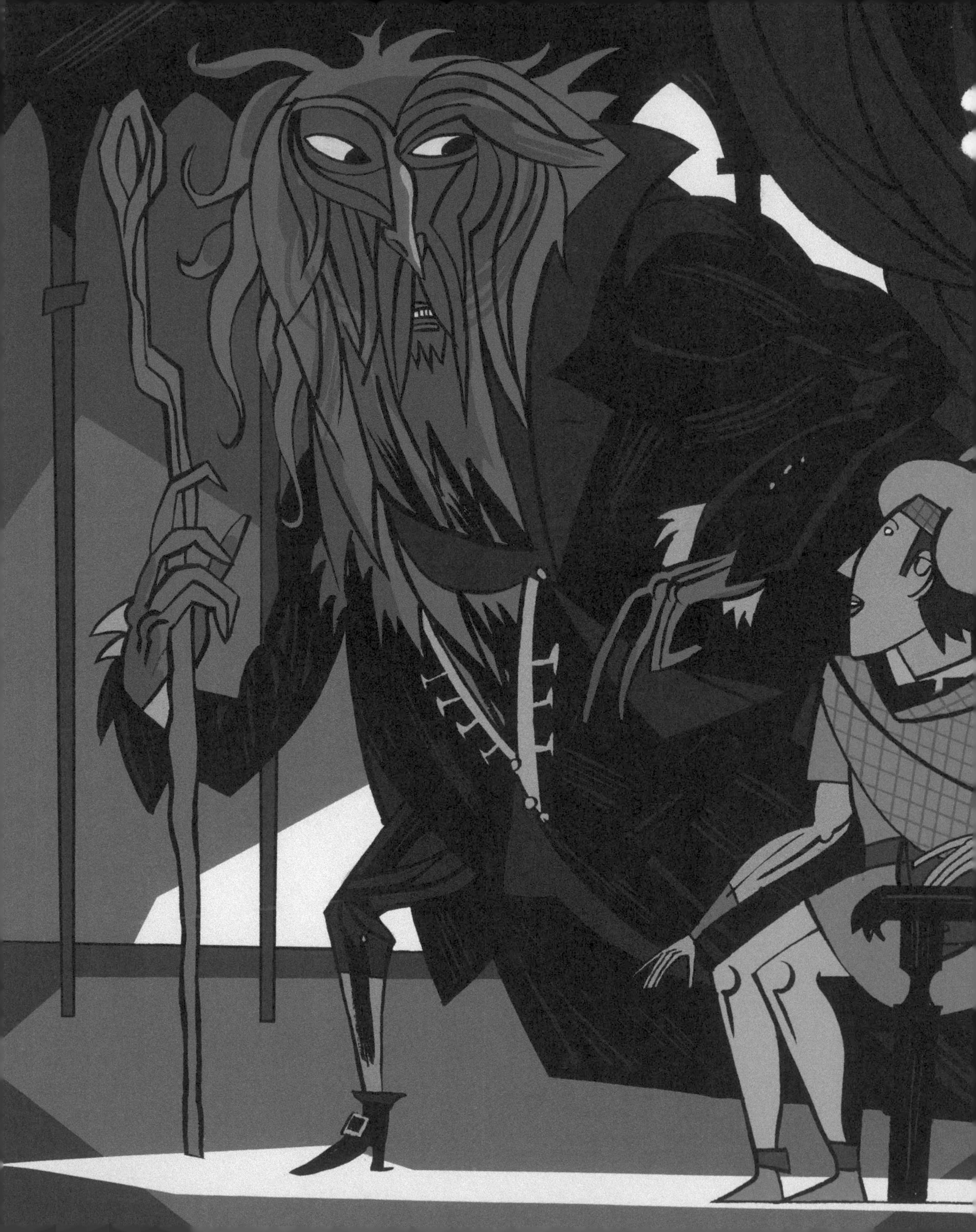

THE DRAIGLIN HOGNEY

Once there lived a poor man in Scotland who had three sons. When his eldest son grew into a young man, he knew that he needed to make his fortune and find his path. Eager to seek his destiny, he asked his father for a horse to ride upon, a hound to hunt with, and a hawk to guide him. With those few things the man could give to accompany him, he ventured out.

He rode over hills through dales, and as the sun was setting, he came to an immense forest. The young man tried to find a path into the forest but became helplessly lost in the dark and shadowed woods. He had almost given up hope of finding his way through when he saw light filtering through the trees.

Making his way foward, he found himself in a clearing where a stately castle stood. With its brightly lit torches flickering, it looked as if a banquet were being held. But the large door was barred shut. He pounded on the door, hoping that someone would answer. It flew open, but no one could be seen.

The young man walked in and wandered from room to room looking for the owners of the castle, but none could be found. Fires were blazing in the hearths, and the halls were lined with flaming torches mounted to the walls. Wandering into the banquet hall, he found a feasting table laid with ham, goose, root vegetables, and berries. So weary and tired was the young man that he placed his horse in one of the stable stalls and took his hound and hawk with him into the hall to eat dinner.

After eating his fill, he sat by the fire. Growing ever groggier, he was awakened by a clock that struck midnight. In a flash, a huge figure appeared in the door, and he found himself face-to-face with the horrible-looking Draiglin Hogney. This man-eating giant had a long, unkempt beard and a mess of greasy and scraggly hair. In his hands, he carried an odd-shaped club.

The giant did not seem surprised to see a guest sitting at his table, and so he sat down and glanced over at the young man. "Is your horse unruly, and does he kick?" he asked.

It was a strange question, but the young man replied, "Why, yes, he does." For his father hadn't fully tamed the horse.

The Draiglin Hogney then laughed and said, "I can tame horses. Take this hair and throw it over him, and he will no longer kick." The ogre picked a long, crooked hair from his own head and gave it to the young man, who went to the stable and did as he was told, almost as if he were under some enchantment.

Sitting again at the table, the ogre asked another question. "Does your dog ever bite?"

The young man replied, "Yes, he does." For his father had not yet trained his hound not to snap and nip at people's ankles. The Draiglin Hogney then pulled another hair from his head and told the lad to throw it over his hound, and so he did this, too.

Lastly, the giant asked, "Does your hawk ever peck?"

The young man replied, "Yes, she does. I have to be careful not to put anything within her reach." For his hawk was quick to peck. The hogney then gave the lad another hair and had him throw it over the bird. Instantly, all the animals turned to stone. The ogre hit the young man on the head with a club and turned him into stone, too.

Back at home, the second of the three sons made a similar agreement with his father. He asked to be provided with a horse, a hawk, and a hound, to which his father agreed. He soon set out to find his fortune. Like his brother, he came to the same woods and became lost only to find himself at the exact same castle. He went inside and ate supper, just as his older brother had. Then the Draiglin Hogney came in and asked the exact same questions. The young man threw the hairs over the animals, turning them into stone. Like his brother, this young man was hit with the club and likewise turned into stone.

Time passed quickly, and soon the youngest son had become a man. Like his two older brothers, he asked for a horse, a hawk, and a hound. However, he didn't desire fortune. He only wanted to find his missing brothers. The old man gave the creatures to his son, who followed in his brothers' footsteps. He traveled the same roads and woods and soon found himself at the same castle.

But unlike his brothers, the youngest son was a cautious lad. He didn't like the uneasiness he felt in the empty castle. Nor did he like the fact that he found a feast set for no one. And he liked the Draiglin Hogney least of all.

So, when the ogre asked him a question, he answered, but when told to throw the hair over the horse he only pretended to do so. The Draiglin Hogney asked the same other questions and plucked hairs for the other animals as well. The young man only pretended to throw the strands over them, too.

The ogre believed that he had this young man in his grasp, too, and the animals under his control. And so he took his club and ran to strike the young man. But the boy's horse, hound, and hawk were alert and aware and very much not turned to stone.

The horse cared much for the young man, and when he saw the ogre about to harm him, he galloped toward the hogney and knocked him down. The hawk flew from the young man's shoulder to scratch the ogre's face. The dog bit the hogney in the leg, and the hogney perished. The young man was safe, and the animals were happy they had saved him.

When the lad looked down toward the ground, he noticed the oddly shaped club and picked it up. Thereupon he decided to explore the castle and found gloomy dungeons beneath. In one of the cells he found the stone figures of his missing brothers, frozen in time.

"Brothers! What happened to you?" he exclaimed.

He bent down and touched them with the club, and to his astonishment, it thawed the stone and revived his siblings. They wept happy tears at their reunion, saying, "This is a glorious day!"

They made their way to another dungeon, where they found stone hawks, horses, and hounds. The youngest brother used the club once again and restored each of them.

At last, they all began to explore the remaining chambers when, lo and behold, they came across two rooms filled entirely with silver and gold coins. It was more than enough to keep and provide an entire kingdom for each of them.

The young men buried the Draiglin Hogney and moved into the castle. They sent for their father, who came to live a prosperous life with his now-wealthy sons. They all continue to live happily in this kingdom even to this very day.

BEHIND THE HOGNEYS, HOUNDS, AND WITCHES— QUESTIONS TO THINK ABOUT

- Can people sometimes take advantage of you as the hogney did the young men?
- Is it wise to trust someone you have just met as the men did with the hogney?
- Can friends (even the animal kind) get us through difficult circumstances?

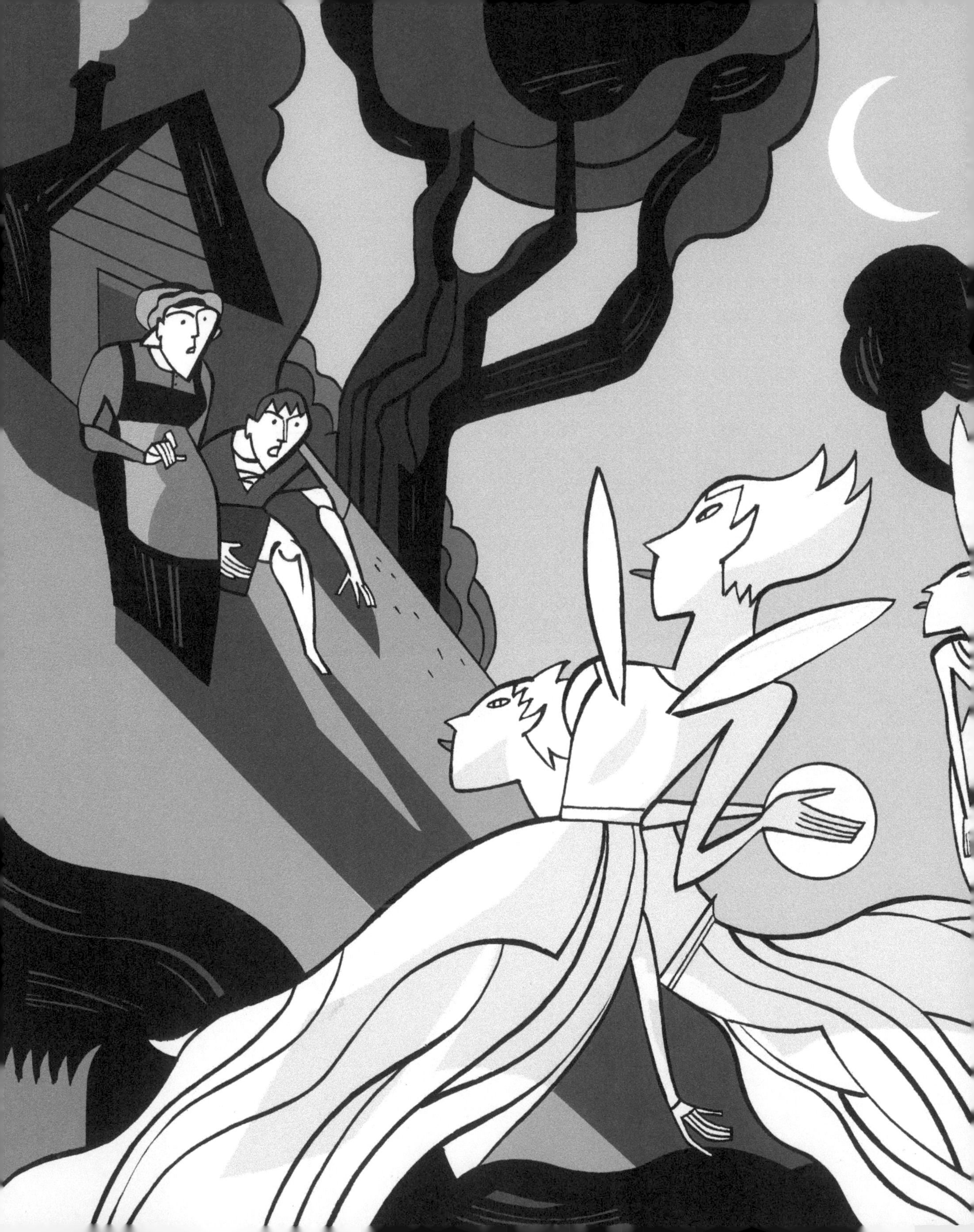

ELIDOR

IN THE KINGDOM OF THE LITTLE PEOPLE

——— *Wales* ———

Long ago during the time of King Henry I of England, there lived a young lad by the name of Elidor. His mother was a widow, but she tried to provide for her son the best she could.

Elidor was being schooled to be a church bishop, which was one of the few positions that provided a good livelihood and education. Every day the young boy would travel from his home to the scriptorium run by the monks.

But the young lad was a bit lazy, and as quickly as he learned one word he would forget another. The monks were quite frustrated. The boy was making very little progress.

One day a monk remembered the phrase "Spare the rod and spoil the child," so the monks tried to make him learn by punishing the boy. Whenever he forgot another word, he would receive another punishment. As time went on, they began to punish him more and more. The boy finally decided that he had had enough of life at the monastery, so he left, journeying far into the immense forest of St. David.

The young lad traveled day and night for two days, but he could not find his way through the forest. He survived by eating rose hips and berries. At last he found himself at the entrance to a vast cave. In front of the mouth of the cave was a rushing river. He grew tired and sat down to rest, but his head dropped off in sleep.

Elidor was startled awake by the sudden appearance of two tiny beings, each no taller than two feet, with bushy beards and jolly features. They said to him, "If you follow us, we will lead you to a place where you can play games and eat wonderful food for as long as you like." Elidor was quite hungry, and the games did sound delightful, so he followed the sprites.

The cave was quite dark at first, but as they descended deeper and deeper, they came to an opening to a vast land of pasture, meadows, mountains, trees, and rivers. This strange place had no sun or moon but was lit by a soft light. In this new odd sky, not even stars were seen, for it was almost always cloudy.

The little sprites brought Elidor to their king. He was slightly larger than the other elfin beings but still no taller than Elidor himself. The king asked, "Why have you come here, boy?"

The lad replied, "I do not like my teachers, and I seek to live somewhere I don't need to go to school." The king chuckled, and they spoke a while longer. The king soon thought the boy a suitable playmate for his own son, so he employed him as an attendant of the prince.

While watching over the young prince, Elidor played all manner of sports and games. What Elidor found most astonishing was how these strange and wonderful little people all rode around on little horses about the size of a large dog.

It was custom, the boy learned, for the creatures to eat only saffron milk and fruit, for they found eating meat to be a terrible thing indeed. These little beings had other odd customs, too. It was a strict law among them that they never tell a lie. They found the world of humans horrid because lying was so frequent among them.

Sometime later, Elidor traversed the passageways in the caves and occasionally saw people of his own size near the mouth. He longed to see his mother again as well as to talk with other townsfolk like himself. He begged the king for permission to go see his mother, which was granted. The little elfin beings led Elidor along the passage back to the human world. They took him through the forest and guided him back to his mother's cottage. She was delighted to see her son.

"Where have you been? I have been worried sick!" she exclaimed and began asking all manner of questions. "Why have you been gone so long? Whom have you been with?"

The young boy told her all about his adventures in the elfin kingdom. His mother begged her son to stay with her, but he could not. Elidor had promised the king that he would return.

Soon the young lad returned to the hidden realm. From that day forward, he spent time in the human world as well as in the land of little creatures, seeking the best of both worlds.

One day, the young lad was with his mother when he mentioned one of the games that he played with the little elves, tossing bright yellow balls. His mother was certain that they must have been made from gold, so she requested that her son bring one home with him on his next journey. She was a poor woman, and surely gold would help their situation.

The boy made his way back to the cave and to the land hidden beyond it. He played games and spent time with the prince, but he soon returned home again, now with one of the golden balls in hand. He quickly ran through the caves and made short work of the journey through the woods. As he neared his mother's cottage, he began to hear the scurrying sound of tiny feet behind him. At that moment, he slipped and fell. The golden ball rolled toward his mother, but as she bent down to pick it up, the little men rushed forward and grabbed it before she could. As they ran off, they stuck out their tongues out at the boy and at his mother, and they disappeared into the forest.

Elidor knew that he had betrayed the trust of the creatures, but he missed his friends terribly. There had to be some way to make it up to them. He hiked through the forest and came near the cave, but the entrance had vanished. Even the river looked different now, taking a different course. Every year the boy went back to see if he could locate the cave, but, alas, it was useless.

After a long while, the young lad decided to go back to school at the monastery. Men came from far and wide there to listen to the story of Elidor in the world of the elves. While he always looked fondly upon his time there, he couldn't help but cry for the loss of his childhood and friends when he left that place.

One day, the Bishop of St. David's made his way to the monastery to hear about the culture of the little people. He wanted to know about the language they spoke. Elidor recounted how the elves would say "udor udorum" when they wanted water and "hapru udorum" when they wanted salt. From this the bishop was able to determine that the beings spoke a form of Greek as in that language "udor" is water and "hap" is salt. But while Elidor found this interesting, he mainly just longed to see his friends again. No matter how much he searched for them, he never did.

BEHIND THE HOGNEYS, HOUNDS, AND WITCHES— QUESTIONS TO THINK ABOUT

- Should Elidor have studied more and not wandered off?
- Why did Elidor betray the elves?
- Can someone make everything right once they have betrayed another person?
- Is it possible to live in two different situations, as Elidor did?

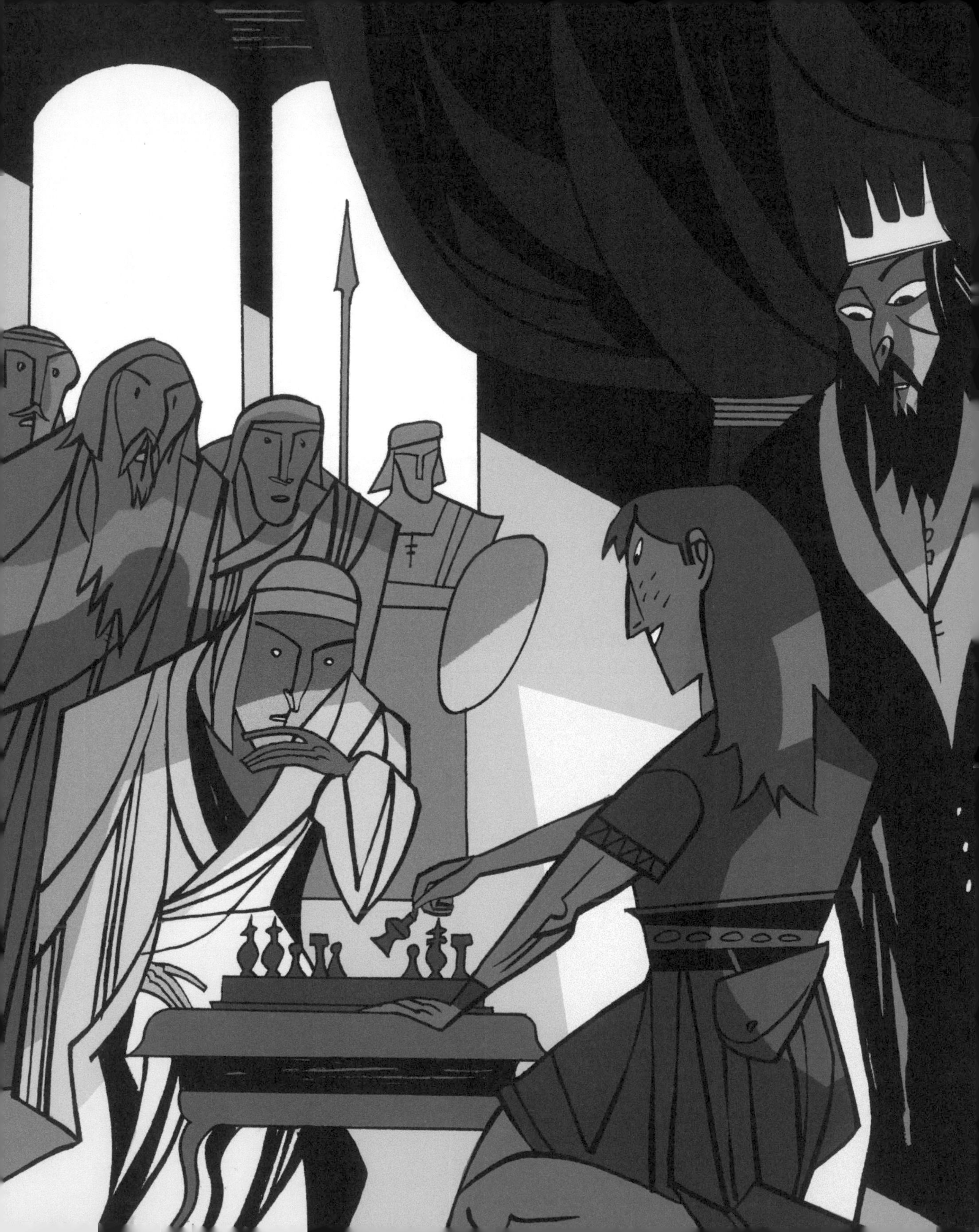

LUGH

Ireland

In the early days of the world, there was a young man named Lugh. He was a tall lad with fair hair and a ruddy complexion. He was a member of two tribes, the son of Cian of the Tuatha De Danaan and Ethlinn, daughter of Balor, King of the Fomor.

However, the young Lugh had trouble fitting in with his mother's people and decided to journey to his father's kingdom to find the great hall of Teamhair (Tara). More than anything, Lugh wanted to have a purpose. He thought, just maybe, he would find a profession and work in Tara. So he saddled his horse and made way for the great hall of Teamhair. Through forests and woods, he made his way to the kingdom. It was a long and challenging journey. Day and night, he traveled. But one day he found himself at the doors of the hall.

Now it was that two men were guarding the entrance to the kingdom. They were Gamal, son of Figal, and Camel, son of Riagal. They were proud and famous warriors with honor and purpose. Lugh admired them. He, too, longed to feel that he had a profession that would give him the same sense of duty. Lugh came forward and asked for entrance into the great hall.

"We cannot let anyone pass without first knowing who you are," replied Gamal.

"I am Lugh, son of Ethlinn, daughter of Balor, the King of the Fomor. My father is Cian of the Tuatha De Danaan."

"That is fine and well," replied Gamal, "but we cannot allow anyone within the great hall who does not have a skill to contribute. What trade are you skilled in?"

Lugh was a bit flustered at this point and took a moment to compose himself. "I am a carpenter. I build all types of furniture and cabinetry. I can be of great use to anyone in the kingdom who has need of such services."

Gamal then replied, "I am sorry, Lugh, but a carpenter already resides within the hall—Luchtar, son of Luachaid. To live here you must have some skill not already provided by those within."

Lugh was disheartened and left the hall in sorrow. However, he had not given up and decided to acquire the skill of a blacksmith. He spent time honing his craft and eventually made his way back to the great hall. He presented himself again to the guards, and they inquired about what trade or skill Lugh was learned in. "I am a blacksmith, and I can help forge anything of metal that the people need." Surely, the boy thought, they would let him in this time. But this was not the case.

Gamal felt terrible for the boy when he replied, "It is unfortunate, Lugh, that we already have Goibhniu, who is greatly skilled in smithcraft."

Lugh was indeed dismayed. Had his long journey to this land been in vain? No, he thought, he had to try once more. He thought about the other skills he possessed. "I am also a warrior," he stated proudly. But, alas, there were also warriors already living in the hall, so this, too, was met with a denial.

Lugh left the hall once again and this time learned several more skills, for one of them had to be needed. He learned to play the harp. He then learned to craft poetry as well as developed the skills of healing and magic. He even went on to learn to work with brass and became a cupbearer. For years he learned these skills, for Lugh knew that one of them had to be of use in the kingdom.

He made his way back to the great hall with many skills in hand. The guards again inquired about the skills he possessed, seeing if any of them were needed. But one by one they denied each and every trade that Lugh had learned until, finally, they came to his utmost skill as a brass worker. This, too, was a skill that was known by someone already living within the hall.

Lugh had nearly lost all hope. There wasn't any other skill that he could think of that King Nuada might need. He sat down for a moment and hung his head in dismay. It had been his dream to live in the great hall, and he had learned every skill known to man, but still there was nothing he could contribute to the kingdom.

Lugh got up and was about to leave when an idea came to him. Individually each trade was represented, but did they have someone who was skilled at all of the professions?

"Go to your king," he asked of Gamal, "and ask him if anyone resides in your kingdom who can perform all of the skills that I have. If there is one among you who can perform all of them, I will leave and ask no more to live among you."

So Gamal went to the king, saying, "There is a young man at the door. He has tried many times before but never presented a skill unique among the people already living here. However, he has acquired every trade known to man and is a master of all arts. Is there anyone living in the kingdom who can claim the same?"

The king thought about it. Surely no one in the land had as many skills as Lugh had mastered. So the king replied, "Go to the young man and take a chess set. See if he can beat you at the game. If so, you may let him through, for no one in this land would be as skilled as he."

Gamal went back to the door carrying a chess set in his hands. The two played for several hours, but Lugh won every single game. At last, the doorkeepers let the young lad through. He made his way to King Nuada's chamber and thanked him for allowing him to live among the Tuatha De Danaan. Just to test the young man's skill, each and every citizen of the land took their talents to challenge Lugh's. Each and every time, Lugh's ability beat their own. He was, indeed, a man of many skills. King Nuada was so impressed by the lad's deeds that he called him Ildánach, a name meaning "many-skilled one."

Lugh was a great asset to the kingdom of Tara. In the battles that were to come, Lugh proved to be a tremendous warrior, well versed in all types of arcane knowledge. He outwitted every foe he ever came up against. Indeed, the title chosen for him by the king—"many-skilled one"—was appropriate. Lugh never stopped learning, becoming ever more adept at the skills that he had already acquired. And this was the story of how Lugh came to live among the Tuatha De Danaan.

BEHIND THE HOGNEYS, HOUNDS, AND WITCHES— QUESTIONS TO THINK ABOUT

- Was Lugh's journey more about discovering who he was than it was about coming to live in a new place?
- What skill allowed Lugh to live within the kingdom? Was it something he learned, or was it perseverance?
- Did the process of petitioning to become a resident of the great hall cause Lugh to become a better person?

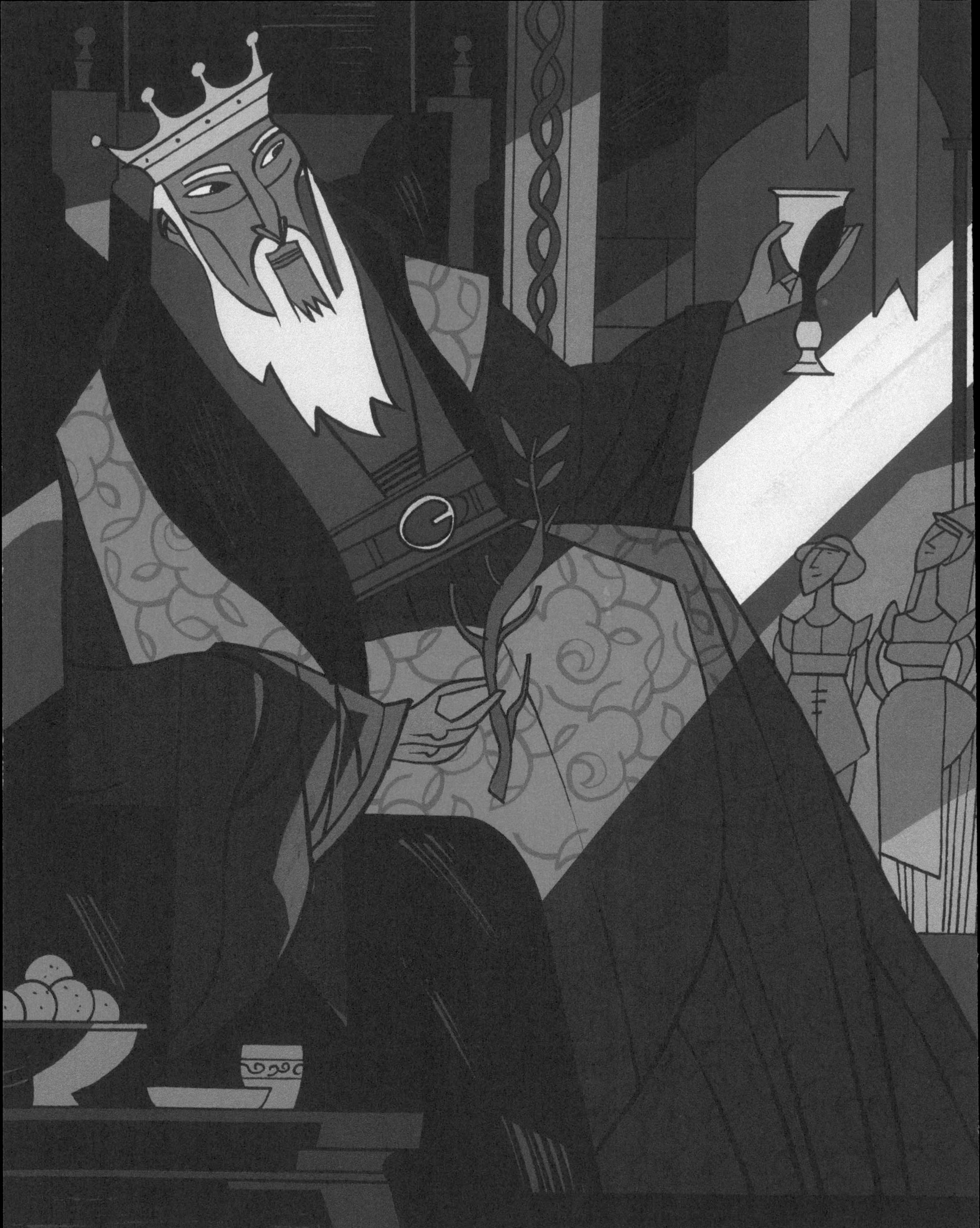

CORMAC AND MANANNAN

Long ago in the country we now know as Ireland lived a young king named Cormac, who was newly named as High King. Although he was now the leader of the land, he was still young, barely more than a child and unaware of the consequences of his actions.

One day he saw a young boy in the pasture in front of the castle. In the youngster's hands was a fairy branch. It gleamed like silver and was festooned with nine shimmering red apples. This, indeed, was an enchanted fairy branch. Every time it was shaken, people around it would forget all of their worries, and some would fall into a deep slumber. Curious, King Cormac decided to mount his horse and ride up to the boy.

As the young king reached the boy, he asked, "Do you own that fairy branch?"

"Yes, good king, I do."

The king was captivated by the sparkling silver bough and asked, "Would you please sell it to me?"

The boy replied with a demand. "I will only sell it if you give me anything that I require."

The king promised to give the young lad anything that he wanted. All he needed to do was name his price. The young lad immediately demanded the wife, young daughter, and baby boy of the king. It was only then that the king truly understood what he had done. But no matter how much the king pleaded, the boy would not budge from his demand. Finally, the king gave in to the youngster's demands.

The wife and children of King Cormac cried as they departed, but the king shook the magical bough, and it took away all of their sorrow. When the people of his kingdom found out that the royal family was missing, great mourning overtook the land. So the king took out the bough and shook it, clearing all of the worry and sadness that clouded his kingdom.

After a year had passed, King Cormac began to wonder how his family was faring. He mounted a horse and took the same path to the west that he had seen them take one year prior. It was not long before young King Cormac encountered a magical mist—a swirl that enveloped him and through which he wandered lost for some hours before he came across a beautiful plain. In the distance, he saw men thatching the roof of a home with what appeared to be feathers—giant and fluffy plumes. They were so massive that the king did not know from what kind of bird they had come, but he knew it was bigger than any he had ever seen. After one side of the house was thatched, the men went to retrieve more feathers, but when they returned, they found that all their work had been undone, and the feathers had all fallen to the ground.

Next, the young king came across a boy dragging trees to throw into a fire. Before the lad could get a second tree into the pit, the first had completely burned away. This seemed to be, as the young king realized, a never-ending labor.

King Cormac traveled farther and discovered three huge wells on the edge of the plain. Within each of wells sat a head. From the mouth of the first head rushed forth a stream that split into two. The second head had a single river flowing out and another one flowing in. Three creeks emerged from the third head. The king watched in wonder for a while and eventually rode forth to a cozy house nearby.

Inside he found a giant couple wrapped in clothing of many colors. They welcomed the king and bid him to stay for the night, and he agreed. The wife asked her husband to bring food to eat. He returned later with a massive boar and a log. He threw them down upon the floor before the king and said, "Here is your food. Now cook it."

King Cormac was stunned. How could he cook such a large swine?

As if reading the king's mind, the giant spoke. "I will teach you how to prepare the beast. Simply split the log into four pieces. Then split the hog into four pieces. Place a piece of wood under each quarter. Once they are all laid out, tell a true story and the meat will be magically cooked."

"Good sir, can you show me?" inquired the king.

So the giant told his story as the first quarter cooked. "I have seven pigs of the same kind. They could feed the world, since when one has been eaten I simply put the bones in the pigsty again and the next morning it will be found alive once more."

The king had heard this story and believed it was true. King Cormac then asked the lady of the house to tell the second story as the second quarter of the hog cooked.

The lady of the house replied, "The seven cows I own fill seven cauldrons with milk each and every day. They could give sustenance to the entire human race." This story also had to be true.

It had now come time for King Cormac to tell his story so that the third quarter of the swine would cook. "I am on a search for my wife, daughter, and son," he said. "One year ago today, a young boy took them away from me."

The male giant laughed and said, "If your words are honest, then you must be Cormac, son of Art, grandson of Conn."

To which King Cormac replied, "I am." In an instant, the third quarter of the pig cooked itself.

"You may now eat your meal," replied the giant.

"This is the first time I have eaten in the presence of only two people," King Cormac said.

"Would you prefer to have three more people join us?" asked the giant.

"If I knew them, certainly I would," the king replied.

Instantly, the door flung open, and in front of him stood his wife and children. The king was elated to have found his family. The spell of enchantment was lifted, and the giant transformed, the Irish Sea God, Manannan Mac Lir, appearing in his place. He said, "It was I, Cormac, who took away your family. It was I who gave you the branch so that I might bring you here. Now eat, drink, and be merry."

"I will happily do so," replied the king. "But may I learn what all of the wonders I saw today mean?"

"Yes, I will gladly tell you. The men thatching the roof were a guise showing you how people go out into the world to seek their fortunes only to return home to find their homes bare," said Manannan as Cormac nodded.

"The boy burning the trees is like those who work for others, earning wealth for their masters but never having any to warm themselves," said the god, as the king nodded. "And the wells showed the three types of people. Some give freely only when they get in equal measure, some give willingly although they get little, and lastly, those who give little but get much. The last is the worst of the three," said Manannan.

King Cormac was quite impressed. Manannan placed his hand in a bag, and out he brought a vessel, one he held in his palm. "This is a goblet of virtue. It falls into four pieces when a false story is told and unifies again once a true story is uttered."

"You show us great treasures, Manannan," said King Cormac.

"I am showing you these items as I am giving them to you."

At last the king and his family sat down at a table with a cloth laid before them. "The cloth before you is a treasure, too, for whatever food you ask of it will be provided," Manannan said.

It was the best meal that the family had eaten in ages, for the food they most desired was provided by the magical cloth. Afterward, the family became weary and soon went to sleep. The next morning, they all awoke back home with the gifts Manannan had given them.

From this encounter, King Cormac gained not only gifts but great wisdom with which he ruled his kingdom judiciously. Once an ill-informed boy, he was now back together with his family and truly a wise man.

BEHIND THE HOGNEYS, HOUNDS, AND WITCHES— QUESTIONS TO THINK ABOUT

- Should the king have bargained without knowing what the consequences were?
- How did King Cormac's journey change him?
- Is wisdom a gift in and of itself?

GLOSSARY

bairn (bayrn): A Scottish word meaning child

Ballyhoura (Bah-ley-hor-a): A mountain range in the southwest of Ireland

bannocks (bah-nocks): An ancient type of cake made of oatmeal

banshee (ban-shee): A female spirit whose shrieks or wails warn of death

bard (bard): A professional storyteller and genealogist

barrow (bear-oh): A small hill in which someone is buried

besom (beh-som): Twigs tied around a stick to make an improvised broom

brownie (brow-ney): A household spirit that performs chores for the occupants

card, carder, carding (card): A piece of wood with wool wrapped around it, which is then separated into individual fibers; the process of separating wool fibers

causeway (cos-way): A roadway or path

craig (crayg): An outcropping of rock or a cliff

croagh (crow): A mountain or hill, often associated with a specific mountain, such as Croagh Patrick

cupbearer (cup-bare-er): A person who serves wine

draiglin (drayg-lyn): Soaking with rain or mud

druid (droo-id): A priest or magician

etin (eh-din): A Scottish word meaning giant, ogre, or devil

fae (fay): The class of creatures that we now call fairies

fianna (fee-an-na): A band of warriors who followed Finn

Finn (Fin): A legendary Irish hero

Gaelic (Gay-lik): The ancient language of Scotland and Ireland

henge (henje): A stone circle

hogney (hoge-ny): An entity with an unkempt appearance

imp (imp): A mischievous sprite

Kirkwall (Kirk-wal): The largest town in Orkney

Kittlerumpit (Kit-ill-rump-it): A fictional city

knocking stone (nock-ing stohn): A bowl-shaped stone in which grain is pounded to remove the hull

leprechauns (lep-reh-cons): Small, bearded men who like to engage in mischief

Lugh (Loo): The Gaelic name of the many-skilled god that may mean "to hold someone to an oath"

moor (mor): An uncultivated area of land

Niamh (Neev): The wife of Oisin, daughter of Manannan Mac Lir, princess of the otherworld

Nuada (Noo-da): The first king of the tribe of gods known as the Tuatha De Danaan

nymph (nimf): Female nature spirits, known for living near streams and rivers.

Oisin (Oh-sheen): A great poet and warrior of the fianna; son of Finn

orra man (or-eh man): A man who takes all manner of odd jobs

púca (poo-ka): A shape-changing fairy that can bring good or bad fortune

roane (roe-ann): Another name for a selkie

selkie (sel-key): A being not unlike a mermaid who can transform into a seal

sidhe (she): The name of the fairies of ancient Ireland

Slievenamon (Slee-ven-a-min): A mountain that is home to witches

smithcraft (smith-craft): Occupations pertaining to working with metal

Tara (Tah-ra): The capital of ancient Ireland

Teamhair (Tou-wer): The ancient name of Tara

troth (trohth): Oath of loyalty

Tuatha De Danaan (Too-a-tha day dawn-on): A tribe of Irish gods

Yule (Yool): A festival roughly corresponding to the holiday of Christmas

RESOURCES

Briggs, Katharine. *Dictionary of Fairies*. New York: Pantheon Books, 1978.

Campbell, John Francis. *Popular Tales of the West Highlands*. 4 vols. Edinburgh, UK: Birlinn Ltd., 1999.

Duquesne University, Gumberg Library. "Gumberg Library Research Guide: Celtic Myth and Legend." https://guides.library.duq.edu/celtic-myth.

Evans-Wentz, W. Y. *The Fairy-Faith in Celtic Countries*. New York: Kensington Publishing Corporation, 2003.

Green, Miranda. *Dictionary of Celtic Myth.* New York: Thames and Hudson, 1997.

Guest, Lady Charlotte. *The Mabinogion*. Mineola, NY: Dover Publications, 2012.

Internet Sacred Text Archive. "Celtic Folklore: Sacred Texts." https://www.sacred -texts.com/neu/celt/index.htm.

Jones, Mary. "Celtic Literature Collective." https://www.maryjones.us/ctexts/.

Kinsella, Thomas, trans. *The Táin: Translated from the Irish Epic Táin Bó Cuailnge*. Oxford, UK: Oxford University Press, 2002.

O Hogain, Daithi. *Myth, Legend, and Romance: An Encyclopedia of Irish Folk Tradition*. Upper Saddle River, NJ: Prentice Hall, 1991.

Williams, Mark. *Ireland's Immortals: A History of the Gods of Irish Myth*. Princeton, NJ: Princeton University Press, 2018.

REFERENCES

Gregory, Lady Augusta. *Gods and Fighting Men: The Story of the Tuatha De Danaan and the Fianna of Ireland.* London: Forgotten Books, 1987. http://www.gutenberg .org/files/14465/14465-h/14465-h.htm#L85.

Grierson, Elizabeth W. *The Scottish Fairy Book.* Sydney: Wentworth Press, 2016. http://www.gutenberg.org/files/37532/37532-h/37532-h.htm#Page_136.

Griffis, William Elliot. *Welsh Fairy Tales.* Fairfield, IA: 1st World Library—Literary Society, 2007. http://www.gutenberg.org/files/9368/9368-h/9368-h.htm.

Hughes, Harold F. *Legendary Heroes of Ireland.* Indianapolis, IN: Palala Press, 2016. https://www.gutenberg.org/files/50490/50490-h/50490-h.htm#ch06.

Jacobs, Joseph, ed. *More Celtic Fairy Tales.* Mattituck, NY: Amereon Ltd, 2010. https://www.gutenberg.org/files/34453/34453-h/34453-h.htm#Page_1n.

Joyce, P. W. *The Wonders of Ireland and Other Papers on Irish Subjects.* Indianapolis, IN: Palala Press, 2015. https://www.libraryireland.com/Wonders /Fergus-OMara-1.php.

Mackenzie, Donald Alexander. *Wonder Tales from Scottish Myth and Legend.* Sydney: Wentworth Press, 2019.

Masson, Elsie. *Folk Tales of Brittany.* Accessed October 1, 2019. https://www .sacred-texts.com/neu/celt/ftb/ftb07.htm.

Spence, Lewis. *Legends and Romances of Brittany.* Accessed October 1, 2019. https://www.gutenberg.org/files/30871/30871-h/30871-h.htm.

Yeats, William, ed. *Fairy and Folk Tales of the Irish Peasantry.* Mineola, NY: Dover Publications, 2011. http://www.gutenberg.org/files/33887/33887-h/33887 -h.htm#Page_59.

INDEX

A

Alfheim, 37–41

B

Ballyhoura Mountains, 83–87
Bards, 37–41
Bella, 43–49
Betrayal, 117–121
Brittany
    La Rose, 63–67
    The Witch of Loch
        Isle, 43–49
The Brownie of Ferne
    Den, 9–13

C

Camel, 123–127
Cormac and
    Manannan, 129–134

D

The Draiglin Hogney, 111–115
Dwarves, 89–93

E

Elidor in the Kingdom of the
    Little People, 117–121
Elves, 37–41, 117–121
Enchantments, 15–21, 23–27,
    43–49, 71–75

F

Fairies, 3–7, 15–21, 51–55,
    57–61, 71–75, 77–81
Fate, 3–7
Fears, 9–13
Fergus O'Mara's Encounter
    with the Barrow Imp, 83–87
Finn, 57–61
Finn Mac Cumhaill, 95–99
France
    La Rose, 63–67
    The Witch of Loch
        Isle, 43–49
Fraukirk, Countess, 89–93

G

Galway, 29–33
Gamal, 123–127
Giants, 103–109, 111–115
The Giant's Causeway, 95–99
Goblins, 83–87
Green fairy, 3–7

H

Harold, Earl, 89–93
Helga, Countess, 89–93
The Horned Women, 23–27
Houarn, 43–49

I

Imps, 83–87
Ireland
    Cormac and Manan-
        nan, 129–134
    Fergus O'Mara's Encoun-
        ter with the Barrow
        Imp, 83–87
    The Giant's Cause-
        way, 95–99
    The Horned Women, 23–27
    Lugh, 123–127
    Oisin and Niamh, 57–61
    The Púca and the
        Piper, 29–33

K

Katherine Crackernuts, 15–21
Kings, 15–21, 71–75, 103–109,
    123–127, 129–134

L

Lanarkshire, 77–81
Land of the Young, 57–61
Lannilis, 43–49
La Rose, 63–67
Love, 63–67
Lugh, 123–127

M

Malcolm, King, 103–109
Manannan, 129–134
Merlin's Craig, 77–81
Morna, Lady, 89–93

N

Niamh, 57–61
Nuada, King, 123–127
Nymphs, 51–55

O

Ogres, 111–115
Oisin and Niamh, 57–61
Orkney, 89–93
Orphans, 43–49
Orra man, 77–81

P

Paul, Earl, 89–93
Pipers, 29–33
Princes and princesses, 15–21
The Púca and the Piper, 29–33

Q

Queens, 15–21, 37–41

R

The Red Etin, 103–109

S

Scotland
    The Brownie of Ferne
        Den, 9–13
    The Draiglin Hogney, 111–115
    Katherine Cracker-
        nuts, 15–21
    The Red Etin, 103–109
    The Seal Catcher and the
        Selkie, 71–75
    Seven Years in Merlin's
        Craig, 77–81
    Snorro of the Dwarf
        Stone and the Two
        Earls, 89–93
    Thomas the Rhymer, 37–41
    Whippety Stourie, 3–7
The Seal Catcher and the
    Selkie, 71–75
Selkies, 71–75
Seven Years in Merlin's
    Craig, 77–81
Siblings, 15–21
Snorro of the Dwarf Stone and
    the Two Earls, 89–93
Sprites, 77–81, 117–121
Stepparents, 15–21, 89–93

T

Thomas the Rhymer, 37–41
The Touch of Dirt, 51–55
Tuatha De Danaan, 123–127

V

Velvet Cheeks, 15–21

W

Wales
    Elidor in the Kingdom of the
        Little People, 117–121
    The Touch of Dirt, 51–55
Whippety Stourie, 3–7
Witches, 15–21, 23–27, 43–49
The Witch of Loch Isle, 43–49

ACKNOWLEDGMENTS

The author would like to acknowledge the many people who played a part in bringing this book to life. First and foremost, he would like to thank his parents, Paul and Diana Pinard, who fostered his love of folklore and mythology. Additionally, he would like to thank his lifelong companion, Kauakea, for being understanding of all the long hours of writing, including late into the night. Additionally, Kauakea has been one of Chris's most ardent supporters with respect to his writing. Thanks also go to the editor of this book, Jesse Aylen, and all those at Callisto Media who helped bring this book to print. Finally, the author would like to give thanks to all of his friends who supported this endeavor, especially the Tea Time Crew (Stephanie Montes, Brianna George, Veronica Renson, Alexandra Broaddas, Gabriela Espino, Molly Ridenour, Nicole Hammond, Sarahanne Alexander, Stacey Bowen, Julie Gonzalez, Pam Voltin, Carla Banducci, Ashley Jones, Jennie Linhares, Jamie Boyer, and Reyna McGuire).

ABOUT THE ILLUSTRATOR

 **Javier Olivares** is an award-winning cartoonist, illustrator, and a professor of the "Escuela Minúscula de Ilustración" ("Tiny School of Illustration"). As an author, his illustrations have appeared in children's books published by SM, Anaya, Media Vaca, Cruïlla, and Santillana, and he has published numerous comic books. His works for the press have appeared in *El País*, *Público*, *El Mundo*, *El Correo*, and the *Boston Globe* newspapers. In 2015, he won the National Comic Award for the graphic novel *Las Meninas*, co-created with Santiago García, and published in the United States by Fantagraphics, where it was nominated for the prestigious Eisner and Ignatz awards. His new graphic novel *La Cólera*, also co-created with Santiago García, has been published in Spain by Astiberri. Javier is based in Madrid, Spain.